WITHDRAWN

Wingtips

JOHNS HOPKINS:

POETRY AND FICTION

JOHN T. IRWIN,

GENERAL EDITOR

|||||||||| stories by
Avery
Chenoweth

Wingtips

THE JOHNS HOPKINS

UNIVERSITY PRESS

BALTIMORE AND LONDON

This book has been brought to publication with the
generous assistance of the G. Harry Pouder Fund.

The Johns Hopkins University Press
2715 North Charles Street
Baltimore, Maryland 21218-4363
www.press.jhu.edu

Library of Congress Cataloging-in-Publication Data
will be found at the end of this book.
A catalog record for this book is available from the
British Library.

ISBN 0-8018-6023-7

"Wingtips" first appeared in *The Blue Moon Review.*

"Born to Run" by Bruce Springsteen.
© 1975 by Bruce Springsteen. Reprinted by permission.

With a tip of the top hat and a thanks to John Barth, Stephen Dixon, and George Garrett for their years of invaluable help, insight, and encouragement

And, of course, with love to K. and A., Richard, Isabel, Matthew, and Katharine, and all the other members of my family, whose humor, compassion, and·storytelling have made much of this fiction possible

We shall not cease from exploration
And the end of all our exploring
Will be to arrive where we started
And know the place for the first time

T. S. ELIOT

One day we'll get to that place
Where we really want to go
And we'll walk in the sun
'Cause tramps like us,
Baby, we were born to run

BRUCE SPRINGSTEEN

|||||||| Contents

|||||||| Powerman

THE ADULTS WHO SAT ON THE VERANDA, SIPPING MARTINIS and talking in the darkness, could not have known they were being watched. He moved inseparably through the shadows under the porch. From beyond the tall doors that opened onto the porch came the sounds of his siblings and cousins playing a board game on the living room floor. The red and blue glass lights of the brass lantern above the circle of adults flashed in the breeze, and under its colors several conversations came together in a burst of laughter. He took a step closer, invisible.

"No, I don't know when he's coming down," his mother went on. "And I don't think this is the time to discuss it, with little Mr. Big Ears around."

"Well, I think it's time for more ice," his Uncle Andrew said, then apparently stood up—a rocking chair swung loose, and heavy steps went inside. It frustrated him that he couldn't see what they were doing up on the porch, only listen.

"Well," his grandmother, Granelle, said, "I just think you two should decide this thing one way or the other. Your father can make arrangements with the schools down there—"

"Mother, please! I'm not going to discuss it right now."

"Mother, for God's sake . . . " Now his Uncle Jack stood up. "Here, let me freshen your drink for you."

"I've just really had it up to here," his mother was saying. "I've been on the phone all day—"

"I'm sorry," his grandmother said. "I just thought that if Jason was still writing you those letters—"

"Mother, drop it, for Christ's sake." Uncle Jack had walked across the porch. "You want tonic water or is soda fine with you? Carol? Let me freshen that for you."

He had heard some of this bickering before, so he did not listen to it now. Rather, he pictured his Uncle Jack standing at the card table, fixing his grandmother's drink. Uncle Jack was a slender young man, cool because he was just out of college, because he wore penny loafers without socks and owned a *Meet the Beatles* album—Beatlemania now entering its last phase—and because he kept a stack of *Playboy* magazines in his bedroom closet.

As the adults argued, he thought how great it would be if he could go and live with his grandparents and Uncle Jack in Jacksonville. His grandparents' house in the drowsy Floridian city was a huge old place surrounded by water oaks hung with rags of Spanish moss, rambling with gables and verandas, rooms ghostly with old portraits, and long dark hallways and vacant bedrooms where the closets were full of clothes and smelled of mothballs—rooms with Persian carpets where he would pull on old, white dinner gloves, tie spats over his sneakers, and stand before mirrors losing their silver. The old house sat beneath trees near the banks of the St. Johns River, where the wind came thick with the smell of fish and brackish tide; and for hours he couldn't count, he had stood in dim hallways staring into old landscape paintings gone dark with aging varnish, dreaming himself into the scenery where the leafy masses of trees opened onto an endless panorama blue as paradise, with the invariable shepherd boy in his straw hat, flock nearby.

Each year the cousins of his extensive southern family came together in this mountain town of Beersheba Springs, Tennessee, on the edge of the Cumberland Plateau, where they vacationed in antebellum summer houses, and this day, like all those of the previous week, had gone well. They went swimming in the river down in the valley. The adults played tennis on the clay court, his Uncle Andrew sporting a new V-neck tennis sweater. After supper everyone, adults and children, took a walk around the loop—an ambling dirt road with deep-porched cottages—and the children ran ceremoniously past the graveyard, its slanting headstones visible back among the trees.

But if the vacation had started well, it wasn't still going that way. For some reason, his mother and grandmother were always arguing, either in quick exchanges like the one above him now or late at night when they met in his mother's bedroom and spoke behind closed doors. Everyone was tired. Just now, in the living room, a quarrel broke out between his siblings. The smack. Two smacks. Brian and Jay shouting, one kicking the other, Jay claiming not to be hurt, then wailing for help.

"I don't think I can stand it a moment longer," his mother said.

"For Christ's sake," Jack said, and his shadow cut across the oblong of light that fell diffusely from the door into the yard.

A separate pair of footsteps came back across the porch. "Well, I found some ice, but it's not much." His Uncle Andrew exhaled heavily, and the wicker and wood of his rocking chair cinched under his weight.

Uncle Jack spoke inside the living room. "I mean it," he went on. "You kids separate. If I have to come in here again, I'll see to it that Mrs. Hillis chops you up and bakes you into a pie. Now, behave. Or better yet, go play Peeping Tom like Stuart. Hey, how about this game—see who can find him. The winner won't get a spanking."

Uncle Jack's girlfriend, Beatrice, swung back in her rocking chair on a gust of laughter, and Stuart glimpsed her beehive hairdo above the railing. She was Jack's girlfriend from Vanderbilt, and really pretty, with frosted pink lipstick and gooey mascara. She also had large breasts that stuck out like missiles.

"Find him," Uncle Jack was telling the children. "I don't know. Go find him."

Pairs of sneakers ran onto the porch, thudded down the steps, and jumped onto the grass, scattering the blue and red lights of the lantern across the yard.

Stuart was gone, flying into the darkness. Behind him on the veranda, Uncle Andrew shouted, "There goes that bear!" and all the adults laughed. When he got to the old, red cedar tree at the end of the driveway, which signaled a place he called the Safety Zone, he stopped, alone and breathing hard.

In the early morning the small cousins would pull on the rope, and the breakfast bell would bing and bang on the dry summer air. The brass ship's bell sat on a hickory post outside the kitchen door, and before it was done ringing, everyone would emerge from their rooms with a rhythm as casual as the sequence of days, cross the back porch, and swing down the back steps to the dining room and kitchen, which stood apart in a separate building. The crowd of first cousins, uncles, and aunts arrived like an occupation army and filled the nineteenth-century kitchen, from its beaded board walls to its torn window screens, with a bright chaos of conversations and preparations that were as traditional as the menu of eggs, grits, and sausage. And here was the source of summer and family for him. For all the collisions between personalities, no one here screamed drunkenly, or wept, or slammed doors, and here discipline did not entail being beaten, cringing, back into a closet. Here you said, "Yes, sir" and "Yes, ma'am," and everything ran smoothly. And it was this sense of peace that he hoped to find if his mother would give him permission to live with his grandparents in Jacksonville. His Uncle Andrew stood over the black iron, wood-burning stove, cracking eggs on the rim of the black iron skillet. The girls set places at the grownups' and children's tables. His aunts told everyone what to do, or almost everyone.

"Stuart—" Uncle Jack pushed him outside with the wooden bucket. Although the year was 1968, their plumbing was only recently installed; the previous summer they had still been using the outhouses, and they one and all stilled preferred to drink the well water. The well housing stood in the side yard, its metal hood curved like a sea horse or a mounted chess piece in one of the Alice books; Stuart cranked its rattling handle until freezing water gushed into the bucket, and it became almost too heavy to lift. He lugged it, though, with both hands, and it swung between his knees, sloshing his shins. On the back porch he raised it to the table and set the battered tin dipper into it, the same bucket and dipper that his grandfather's generation had used; and because his grandfather had filled it at Stuart's age, Stuart did so as well. Brian carred in an armload of kindling for the kitchen stove. Jay rang the breakfast bell again, this time for Beatrice who hadn't come down yet. Back in the dining room, the girls carried in platters of food. The boys carried in pitchers of orange juice. To a cacophony of scraping chairs, they sat to eat. And for the next hour, as they made plans for the day, a column of sunshine blazed slowly down the whitewashed bricks of the chimney and spilled evenly across the warm, wooden surface of the grownups' table.

Stuart sat at the children's table where he made sure all the kids got one bowl of Cap'n Crunch. "You got enough," he told Brian, and cracked his brother's knuckles with a spoon.

"What do you think of that, son?"

"Stuart," his mother said. "Your Uncle Andrew is trying to tell you something."

"You tell Brian if he hits me one more time, I'm going to smash his stupid face in."

"He hit me first," Brian said.

Uncle Andrew set his newspaper hard on the table. "Son, don't make me have to come down there."

The other children finished, and Stuart's cousin Betsy—the only other child his age—made them take their plates into the kitchen. The children swung outside through the screen door, where the breakfast hour was already dissipating into the rising heat. His Uncle Andrew made a comment on some new development in Vietnam and passed the paper to Jack.

"What I was trying to tell you a moment ago," he said, "is that Robert and Harry'll be down this coming Saturday. Maybe they'll take you for a hike to Bat's cave."

"But, God knows, you can't act like a little pill," Uncle Jack said. "Or they might just leave you there."

"Hardy-har-har." Stuart turned the red and blue pages of his *Spiderman* comic book.

"Jack, please don't add to it," his mother said. She raised her hand like a crossing guard's stop signal.

"Carol, you know he gets it from his father—" Jack said.

"That's enough of that," his grandmother said. "Now those boys are going to need someplace to sleep, and I'm going to put them down in the little cabin. Now, Stuart, don't interrupt."

He was trying to tell her that he wanted to sleep down in the boys' cabin.

"Well, first, I want you to help Jack put a new roof on it this week," she said. "It leaks, and—"

"Well, can I go and live with you and Papa and Uncle Jack in Jacksonville?" An image of the ghostly old house by the St. Johns' River arose in his mind, bringing with it a vague, romantic mood and a memory of rooms filled with daydreams. "Why not? I'll behave! If it was Moriah, you'd say 'yes.'"

"Because I said so, that's why. Your mother needs you at home to help her when school starts—"

"Oh, wow, some vacation," Stuart said. "Let's pick on Stuart. Do Brian and Jay have to work? No, not them. They get to ride the trolley. They get to go outside and play. And Moriah gets to go to Keystone. Not me. I have to be a good little boy and do all my stupid chores."

"Son," His Uncle Andrew lowered the newspaper, again severe. "Now, son, you're old enough to start helping around here. You're too old to be playing in the sandbox with those children. All you do is get into fights. You do what your grandmother tells you to, and I don't want to hear any more back talk. Is that clear?"

"What was that?" his mother said.

"Aye, aye, captain." He gave the adults a sharp salute.

"You may be excused, young man," his mother said.

He slumped tragically outside—careful not to let the screen door slam—and into the pointless heat.

The afternoon went as Stuart could have predicted. The work was boring and hot and stupid and dull and dumb.

"I didn't ask if you liked it, you little smartass," Jack said. "Just get me that bucket of nails. Don't make me get off this roof and get them. You just move along and do as I tell you to."

As Stuart crossed the yard, he sullenly watched his little brother ride the trolley—and Brian got a great ride. He leapt way out from the step ladder propped against the hemlock tree, grasping the steel handles, and the T-bar contraption went singing down the wire, with Brian swinging his feet. Coming fast on the tree at the other end, he kicked hard and went lurching and rolling back up the wire. In disgust, Stuart hauled the bucket off the tailgate and lugged it with both hands back across the yard toward the boys' cabin, which sat in the shade of the woods. Jack sat perched on the roof, flipping the hammer by its handle. Rung by rung, Stuart clunked the bucket up the ladder, then raised it uncertainly up to Jack's hand.

"Good Lord," Jack said. "Listen to you whimper. Someone would think you were being tortured."

"Well, I am," Stuart shouted. "I'm tired. That thing's too heavy for me; I told you that. It's easy for you 'cause you're twenty-one, but I'm hardly even eight. I can't carry that thing. It must weigh fifty pounds."

Jack smacked the claws of the hammer under a tier of rotten shingles. He jerked his elbow down, and tar paper and nails came wrenching up. When he had torn them off the roof, he spun them scattershot, like broken frisbees into the the surrounding branches. Stuart hung from the ladder in a state somewhere between protest and boredom. The two of them paused, and the summer had its effect; they became alive to the world beyond their work. The morning was sounding with incidentals: the clacking of a screen door, voices and footsteps on the back porch, and, somewhere, a motorcycle roaring away into the distant mountain silence. In the next moment they were uncle and nephew again, and Jack was wrenching loose another handful of old green shingles.

"Hey, let me throw some." Stuart leaned back on the ladder, yanking it off the gutter. "Hey, can I come live in Jacksonville with you guys? Mom won't let me."

"No."

"Why not?"

"Not until you stop being such a little pissant all the time and help around here. I was appalled by that fight yesterday. You should never hit your brother like that."

Stuart let the ladder bang against the gutter.

"Knock it off," Jack said. "Your mother needs you to be very good right now."

"Why?"

"None of your business."

"Tell me."

"When you're older."

"Tell me now," he said, "or maybe I'll just move the ladder."

Jack appeared to smile as Stuart pulled the ladder away from the roof, but the glance over his shoulder was unamused.

"Don't be a little pecker all your life."

"I'll tell Mom you called me that."

Jack ignored him, and Stuart let the ladder slam the gutter.

In the warm hours of afternoon, the children were taken swimming, ostensibly to entertain them but more pointedly to give a few of the adults a rest. Jack drove the station wagon down the serpentine mountain road into the valley, where after miles of nursery farms, they turned in at a white farm house, bounced back through acres of feed corn, and parked in tall grass. "Down scope!"—and the back window rolled into the tailgate. Those not wearing suits changed in a dry but sweltering tool shed dusty with spidery filaments and disuse. Then they came down the hill to the wooden raft, which was roped to a tree. The impact of their feet upon the boards produced tones from the buoyant steel drums, and with the pulley clanking and splashing, the boys hauled on the water-springing rope and brought the raft out from under the shade of slanting trees into the bright silence, the green abstraction of water and sunlight. Inner tubes slapped musically on the water, and the first to dive in always came up shouting and wild about how cold it was. They were always amazed. They seemed always to have come swimming in this long green pool, this bend in an otherwise forgettable river. Theirs was an immutable fall of generations, of uncles and fathers and great-greats, beginning back a hundred years and all landing on the traditional raft to stand on adolescent legs, shivering and skinny, shouting and swimming across an echo of summers.

"Aren't you going to get in?" Floating in an inner tube, Betsy held onto the raft, kicking slow spirals with her feet. "Here, you can have my tube," she said and rolled out.

"In a minute." Stuart sat, chin on his knee, one foot in the water.

But Betsy wouldn't let him alone and the other kids began to tease

him, so Stuart splashed his arms and legs—imitating his grandfather
—and hopped into shallow water in his sneakers and, with a pinch-
hold on his nostrils, dipped himself completely.

After an hour in which he and Betsy piled river stones onto the
walls of the baby pool in the shallows, they found themselves drifting
to the far end of the pool. They held onto each other's inner tubes. A
kingfisher clipped the water and swept into the trees. A horsefly
buzzed them. They seemed to be floating on a surface of green glass,
scratched by an occasional yellow leaf. Over the last ten days they had
begun to spend their evenings flipping through old *Life* magazines
under a bright lamp in the living room, and they were not brother and
sister so they liked each other. Now they were floating within sunlight
and privacy—the other children upstream in the shallows, the adults
on the raft in sunglasses, a cow crashing through the woods back into
the field—and having never felt so intensely alone with a girl, Stuart
heard himself telling Besty all about Powerman and his mission to spy
on the adults. "And especially on Uncle Jack," he finished. "He's always picking on me."

"Oh, wow," Betsy said. "I love to play spy."

And so that night, after the supper plates were carried in, they
slipped away and began. The adults were on the front porch, drinking
and talking, his mother blowing her nose and Uncle Jack announcing
that he and Beatrice were going for a walk around the loop. Betsy and
Stuart sneaked into Great Aunt Mary's bedroom, in the back of which
was the large linen closet. They closed the linen closet door, and by a
moonlit frame of window, they pulled off their clothes to reveal their
bathing suits. Stuart had seen Betsy in her bathing suit before, of
course, but now seeing her body in the silver dark made him feel
weirdly great to be with her, and he awakened to an excitingly illicit
quality of the game. They swung blue and red towels around their
necks, which they clipped on with pink-capped safety pins. Next, they
slid silver soup cans up their biceps to receive superpowers from
starlight; then they leaned out the window, shimmied down the lin-
den tree, and dropped not quite soundlessly onto the gravel drive.
Across the yard they ran, capes flying. They hit the deck. Powerman
waved, and they ran crouching along the picket fence. Figures could
be seen walking in the road—Jack and Beatrice, who vanished into
the dark. The spies came to a stop. Powerman double-tied the knots of

his P. F. Flyers, then checked his Johnny Quest decoder ring. Powergirl, a little bored with him, went on ahead; then they ran quietly out
of the Safety Zone and slipped down the grassy margin of the woods.

They walked for half a mile, passing summer houses where the
brass lanterns on the verandas were turning slow jewels of light and
where adults could be heard talking and laughing. On one porch an
old victrola was scratching Fats Waller's songs out into the cricket-
loud darkness. "It's a lovely night to spoon / Let's pretend that there's
a moon. . . . "

"Look," Powergirl said.

The night was shot with stars that glittered in colors—blue, red,
and gold—down to the tree line. Powerman tried to explain that he
was really from another planet—that, if Stuart wasn't, then Powerman was. "You lie," Powergirl said, and for one bad moment he felt
that this was not the same game for both of them.

They stopped. The antebellum houses were behind them now, and
the solitary street light at the old hotel didn't reach any farther,
though it ran their shadows before them in thin lines over the road
and into the mass of dark which sat hunched before them like an ogre.
They decided to call it a night.

A woman coughed.

They didn't move. She coughed again—and this time, no question,
it came from the town's old graveyard.

"You first," Powergirl said.

"You—" But Powerman stepped across the ditch and moved im-
perceptibly through the grass. He kneeled at the fence of split rails,
which smelled of cedar. Powergirl crouched beside him.

The trees made a canopy against the brightness of the moon, but
Powerman's eyes soon began to adjust. Two people could be seen, on a
tomb. One head, a hand on a back, then one lump moved and the
other head appeared. The heads came together, one at the other's neck,
then mouth to mouth, and on a lift of wind came wet sounds. The figure became a blur. Down at the hotel, a screen door clacked; a motorcycle roared away. Then, on the wind, came the scratch of a zipper, two
zippers. Maybe. He couldn't see them now at all; they had lumped
over on the slab. The safety pin was cutting across his Adam's apple
when Powerman realized that Powergirl was pulling on his cape, and
unable to distinguish anything more, he rose and went away with her.

The children swung the rope, the breakfast bell binged and banged, and August ripened in green warmth and wind. The building projects were moving along simultaneously. The cabin roof and the baby pool were almost finished now beneath the incessantly buzzing song of insects in the sky and woods around them. Rolls of tar paper went down, rocks were gathered, shingles slid and slapped; the pounding of Jack's hammer made dry percussions against the side of the house, and Stuart cradled smooth river stones onto the walls. Everything was not peaceful, however; their mother would frequently remain in her room, and in their efforts to see her, Stuart and his brothers would get into scrapes with each other. The afternoon when he punched his little brother Jay in the shoulder, his grandmother, Granelle, sent him up to the attic, where the boys shared a communal room and where Stuart went quite happily and threw himself out across the sunny, unmade bed to lounge over another *Spiderman* comic book. Within a few lines, however, he was daydreaming out the window, and what began as an almost ineffable sensation of success crystalized with the light in the leaves into a more vivid impression of himself in Jacksonville as a dashing young man, one who would find the love of his life and become rich and famous, so much so that all his tormentors, here and in school, would bow in abject submission whenever he was around. In a while he got bored, went downstairs, and found the stillness of another century.

The adults had found their own escape into the brittle pages of paperbacks, which they read in hammocks and rocking chairs until sleep overtook them. Jack and Beatrice slipped away for a long hike through the woods to Stone Door, a towering cliff that would give them a romantic view of the converging valleys of Savage Gulf. On afternoons when things were really boring, or when the rain fell with a sensuous monotony of steady drumming on the tin roof, Stuart and Betsy would pull out the old Edwardian costumes from the sea chest in the attic and dress themselves in the various velvet pantaloons, vests, and top hats that his grandparents and their guests had used when they performed summer plays back before the First World War. He and Betsy, thus attired as a fop and a fool, would stage dramatic sword fights, using a pair of tennis rackets, until Jack caught them and raised hell. The days were long. The summer afternoons were shapeless, continuing present time, punctuated by the listless slap of a screen door and the way light hung in leaves along the green, cool limit of the woods.

"I don't care who started it, mister. I told you to go to your room right now. Stuart Goodpasture, don't you dare talk back to me. I said now! Mother, would you handle them? I don't think I can stand it . . . " She pressed a wad of Kleenex to her nose, walked to her room, and shut the door.

"You go and do as your mother tells you." Granelle was furious with them. "Don't be such an infernal nuisance that no one wants you around. Well, you are. You don't help. You don't pick up after yourself. You talk back. You pick and quarrel and torment each other so. I don't see how your mother stands it. No," she went on, "I don't know when your father's coming down, and don't ask your mother; she's resting. Now, you get on out there and help Jack with that roof so I have some place to put those boys on Saturday. Now, go on, and don't hit your brother. Brian's not bothering you. He is *not* laughing. Damn a mouse, I never saw such disagreeable children in all my life!"

Evening came. Twilight poured a slow shadow from the mountain over the valley, lighting the eastern range with sun, and spreading a blanket of soft blue silence across the rows of field corn that were fanning by the open windows of the station wagon. The children were cold and wet and quiet. They sat blue-lipped, wrapped in towels. No one talked. There had been a fight down on the raft an hour earlier, when Jack had grabbed Stuart from behind and launched him, screaming, off into the cold, green water. And now he rode in back, watching Jack's profile as the man gazed across the fields. Stuart understood why Jack had thrown him in.

Sometime earlier in the afternoon, when the children were hunting for arrowheads in the plowed ruts of the field, and while the adults were murmuring or sleeping on the raft—his mother as lovely as a movie star in her dark glasses—Stuart had escaped and floated to the far end of the pool. There he had slipped out of the inner tube and waded to the bank of green plants. Kneeling, he sipped at the mouth of the spring, tasting the cold, delicious water, then heard something stepping through the woods, something sneaking not quite soundlessly through the leaves. He looked up. The creature was not a stray cow from the field. It was Jack and Beatrice, brilliant, naked, and stepping through the sunlight.

On the raft a little later, Jack grabbed him hard around the ribcage and threw him aloft, twisting and shouting; the water smacked him, punched the air out of him. Shivering and crying, Stuart dog-paddled back to the raft. He hung on, but his arms were too weak to lift him onto the deck of adults. Jack hauled him up by the wrist.

"You little bastard!" Stuart shouted, cowering in his red towel.

"Jack, for Christ's sake," his mother said. "I asked you not to torment him." She pushed up her dark glasses.

"Me? You know where he gets that language!"

"For God's sake," his grandmother said. "Jack, you behave as badly as he does. Yes, you! You act as through you were twenty-one going on twelve, picking on him like that. Now, you two separate. And, Stuart, you can just go sit in the car until you learn to control that tongue of yours. Now, go on, get."

The subdued atmosphere after the fight followed them up the mountain but broke against the bright porches and activity in the kitchen. Supper was under way, guests were over, and the shaking of martinis under the flashing colors of the lantern out front on the veranda promised an excellent night for spying.

"Well, we're going for a little walk around the loop," Uncle Jack told the others on the front porch.

Powerman and Powergirl dropped from the window of the linen closet into the partial moonlight. Their towels fell over their faces. Jack and Beatrice were going out through the front gate. The spies ran through the woods, on a trail, ahead of them.

Within ten minutes they were in place and trying not to breathe. Powerman lay on his back beneath the stone slab of ELIJAH TATE, 1828 TO 1901, a man of such local power that he alone commanded a monumental site, where the earth had sunk away leaving a bed of old leaves. Powerman shifted his position and the dry rot crunched; the odor of earth and leaves was sharp and unbreatheable under the stone lid so close to his head; vandals must have moved the slab wide enough for him to slip in like this. That must be them. Voices were coming down the road. He almost climbed out for air, but couldn't do that now. They were coming into the graveyard. And as Stuart had discovered that morning, there was only one slab where they might sit, and it had to be this one with the foil packets on the ground. The footsteps stopped and voices murmered.

They were goofing around, stumbling over rocks. Now they sat above him. The backs of their calves blocked his view. Khakis scratched about on the stone surface. Beneath Jack and Beatrice, between their pairs of legs, Powerman's eyes gleamed out in the dark, straining to see up.

"Mmmm. I missed you," she softly said. "All day long I just wanted to kiss you."

Ruffling. Quiet. Down by the hotel a car thundered by.

Unable to see them, Powerman's keen mind began to wander. In one of his outings before Powergirl came along, Powerman had kneeled at the door of the big bathroom and put his eye to the skeletal keyhole. The keyhole made a figure eight of dark inside of which he saw the scene of Beatrice bathing herself in the deep, claw-footed tub. All he could see of her was her face, shoulders, and bare arms. Her hair was pinned up. She raised one leg so she could draw the sponge slowly up the back of her calf. Then she stood, and her breasts rose from the water, her belly, and she was amazing—a dark brush between her legs—some streaming, wet goddess who made him yearn for what he could not yet imagine. Later that night Granelle would lecture him about bothering Beatrice, assuring him that one day he would marry someone just like her, a young beauty in Jacksonville, perhaps. "What the hell are you doing?" Jack knuckled him on the head. "Get out of here—go on, get!" Powerman ran off, but stopped to watch Jack go into the bathroom.

"That better?" Uncle Jack said above him, in the graveyard.

Powerman blinked away the memory of her lovely form rising from the water, of her lovely body striding freely through the green sunlit woods, and so many other moments as well—the way she tossed a ball in tennis, closed a book, jumped up the stairs; the way she dove in, rode a horse, and went for hikes; and most of all that coy glance that made his uncle blush as she asked him for the bacon platter every morning. All he could hope for now was that Powergirl was in place. Jack and Beatrice were making soft noises without talking. Then, the scratch of a zipper. Maybe two.

Powerman slipped his hand up through the breach between the slab and its foundation. His fingers touched Beatrice's thigh. He couldn't think; he was faint. Up above, she moaned. A hand came down on top of his, hard like Jack's, and then another, soft like hers. Jack and Beatrice looked down between her legs and saw a small white hand rising from the grave.

A half mile away on the porch of the family house, Uncle Andrew was going on about how he had somehow managed to splash his khakis with white paint, when he set his drink down on the arm of his rocking chair.

"Listen. Down by the hotel." They all heard it.

"Good Lord," his mother said. "Sounds like all bloody murder's broken loose." She and grandmother left the porch to go put on their sweaters.

In the graveyard Beatrice was screaming. Uncle Jack was screaming. Someone else was screaming like a girl. They stumbled over roots and headstones, hounds were baying, and someone ran crashing into the woods. Down within the tomb Powerman was screaming too. All he heard was his own shrieking laughter against the stone above him. But somewhere down the road, Jack began yelling, "Very funny, you little bastard. We'll talk about this tomorrow."

Powerman laughed, clunked his head against the slab, rolled out of the grave, and stood up amid the tilting headstones. "Got you good, boy," he said out loud, to his imagined audience. A bit nervously he brushed the broken leaves off his legs, suit, and cape and, in case the dead were not dead, jumped onto the dark road and hurried on back to the house.

Powergirl was gone. She was not behind the big tree or the monument from which she was to have appeared as a ghost with arms raised. He called her name, but there was only the steady, unquiet darkness. He passed the summer houses, laughing, shivering, and looking around for Jack. But Jack didn't appear, and as Powerman kept going and began to calm down, he became aware of the smell of damp grass in the night air. It would be September in another week. School would start. He could already see the lumbering yellow school buses, the red and yellow New England trees, the social maneuverings of the hallways, and these things filled him with an excitement and a sadness as quickening as the chill in the woods.

As he came through the side yard, he saw a thin edge of light between the tall louvered doors of his mother's bedroom. Powerman chinned the railing, kicking and scraping the slats of the house with the grass-stained toes of his sneakers. He hung onto the window frame, with his toes jammed into corners between slats. He was about to call out, "Hey, Mom, guess what I did to Uncle Jack!" But the sight in the room stopped him.

His grandmother and mother were shoulder to shoulder on the edge of the bed, blue and red in their sweaters. The reading lamp fluttered moth shadows high into the corners and around the heavy, dark furniture. Granelle was massaging his mother's back. His mother pressed a Kleenex to her nose.

"I don't have a job or credit with the bank. Everything's in his name . . . " She wiped her nose again.

"You knew this was going to happen when you came down," his grandmother said. "All that shouting and profanity. Damn a mouse, I don't see how you could stand it. The children can stay with us. We'll put them in school in Jacksonville while you two settle this thing."

His mother cried like a girl into her Kleenex and said something about the house.

"Let him have the house, if he wants it," his grandmother said. "You never liked the house anyway."

"Not even the goddamn car's in my name!" His mother plucked a Kleenex from the box on her lap. "When I think of how things might have been if Rosaline had just minded her own goddamn business, how happy we might all be right now—"

"That was a long time ago, and they wouldn't even be your children. Now hush—"

"Well, sometimes I think, this time I'll write back, this time I'll do things differently. The next time Jason writes—"

"Don't you answer even one of his letters, you hear me?"

They continued discussing the details, but Powerman's arms were weakening quickly, and they suddenly relaxed and let him fall to the ground. The house seemed to vault above him, vanishing once more above his range of observation and comprehension. Powerman landed with his fingers pressed in the dirt for balance and his cape down over his face. He rose up, tossed his cape into position down his back, brushed off his finger tips, and began to walk very deliberately and slowly around the side of the house. He felt very weak. As he came around to the front porch he broke into a run, but his legs were going on him and he had scarcely reached the sandbox for his ceremonial leap when he heard his Uncle Andrew bellow, "There goes that bear again," and all the adults laughed along with him. Powerman missed the far side of the sandbox wall, tripping into the yard, but continued on, slowing down with each step until he staggered into the Safety Zone, where he was supposed to be beyond the reach of everything that could wound him.

He walked to the old cedar tree, plunked himself down on the grass, and soon fell onto his back, with an arm hooked over his face. He was breathing slowly, taking nothing in but the chill of the night and the way the grass made his bare legs itch. Then it hit him. He caught his breath and began to cry, coughing his guts out. As if from another position, somehow in the air above him, he felt as if he were rising slowly into the branches of the tree above him and, rising farther, was seeing down below him a silly, stupid kid wearing a bathing suit and a towel. Whatever of himself he had put into being Powerman was gone. It hit him again. Stuart cried openly but silently for a long time.

The kids pulled the rope, the breakfast bell banged, and everyone came into the kitchen.

"Well, look who's here. Come on in, boys. We're just about to have some breakfast. Betsy," his Uncle Andrew said, "how about setting two more places at the big table, will you, please?"

Two boys, of perhaps fourteen and fifteen, came in out of the sunlight and created a sensation in the dining room. Their hair was long, and they wore blue jean bell-bottoms and tie-dyed tee shirts. They were from up north and looked like a pair of high school radicals, all of which was new to Stuart. With the men they shook hands; with the women they hugged.

His grandmother, seated at the head of the table, took Stuart by the hand. "I've had these two working all week on the roof of the little cabin down there so you boys can stay down there. You know where the sheets and pillows are."

They were all standing and talking, perhaps twenty of them now, bringing in chairs, finding places at the table. Betsy took down extra plates from the Dutch cabinet. Brian fished utensils out of the tray.

They were loud and gregarious, with the screen door springing open, clacking shut, and others coming in.

Stuart's mother encircled his waist with her arm. He looked at her, the first time that morning. She wore dark glasses; her nostrils were red.

"How would you like to go to school in Jacksonville?" she said.

Stuart couldn't answer. "No," he said, finally.

"You could live with Granelle and Papa and Uncle Jack. Wouldn't that be fun?"

"Hey, man, you want to go?" Harry said from across the table. Although Harry and Robert had just arrived, they already had big plans for the day. "Robert and I are going down to see that barn that Mitchell's building. Maybe we can ride some of his horses."

"Or throw apples at them or something," Robert said.

The other boys laughed.

Betsy said she wanted to go but was told she had to help do laundry and make beds.

Stuart pulled his mother's hand off his waist. "Okay," he said. "Yeah."

"Oh, he's my baby boy," his mother said and pulled him back into a big hug. The adults laughed.

"I said get off, Mom." Stuart pulled loose and stomped into the kitchen. He opened the refrigerator. Someone walked behind him, and he was cracked on the head with a big spoon. He turned to curse; Beatrice was leaving the kitchen with a platter.

After breakfast they stood around the jeep in the driveway, waiting for Stuart to come. He ran out of Aunt Mary's bedroom and, before jumping off the porch, fast-balled a red towel into the wicker laundry hamper.

"Hey, Robert, whittle me a sword," Betsy said. She leaned against the jeep's hood.

Robert flipped the limb of red cedar and caught it. "Sure. Tree out there's almost dead anyway. You can have this one when I'm done."

"Hey, Stuart," Betsy said, as he ran down. "Robert's going to whittle me a sword so we can play pirate."

Stuart climbed in back of the jeep with other male cousins, sat within the coil of rope on the corrugated floor, and looked at the deserter. "You're a little chicken pecker."

The boys in the jeep laughed with him.

"I'll tell your Mom you called me that," she said. Stuart grabbed the frame bar as the jeep accelerated down the gravel driveway under trees and sunlight.

"I'll make you a sword," he shouted.

The rest of that week before Labor Day, when school began, Betsy staged pirate duels with Brian, who was pretty good with a tennis racket. The evenings were chilly, everyone wore cotton sweaters, and one night they built a fire and closed the living room doors. The sight of everyone there in the high-ceilinged room—with the fire blazing, the kids around a board game on the floor, and the grownups reading—made Stuart want to go in there with them, but he remained out in the side yard by the well house. Betsy sat curled on the sofa under a tall lamp, paging through an old *Life* magazine with Stuart's big sister, Moriah, who had arrived that day. The other kids were playing Monopoly and quarreling. Granelle's head eased to one side against the cushion of the chair, and his mother's head fell back, so he knew they must be snoring. His Uncle Andrew, in his paint-splashed khakis, said something, and both women sat forward briefly before closing their eyes again. Jack and Beatrice left for a walk an hour ago, but he hadn't bothered to follow them.

Stuart slapped at his ankles. He had stopped while on a run to swipe a couple of cans from Jack's sixpack in the fridge. Robert and Harry, who had set up their own mission control in the boys' cabin, were letting him sit in on their poker games and uninformed sexual conversations, as long as he stole the beer. They told him that he would like Florida next week—it was so warm and the girls were so great—which allayed his fear of wandering unattached among new kids. Standing there in penny loafers without socks, he slapped at the no-see-'ums biting his ankles, and again a sad damp chill of the woods mingled with an inarticulate excitement for what was coming next and made him want to keep going forever. He thought of barging into the Monopoly game, of just going in there with everyone; but he went on to the kitchen, instead, where he flipped on the light and let the screen door slap behind him.

|||||||| Housework

THAT WAS THE GREEN AND GOLDEN SUMMER I SPENT ON Martha's Vineyard, drifting at night in clouds of beautiful people and by day cleaning the immaculate summer houses of the newly rich. I had come to the island for a weekend visit with college friends, but the allure of ocean twilights and lovely women was too strong for my sense of etiquette, and I stayed on indefinitely. The days went by. Some days I worked, most days I didn't. For two weeks I crashed on their living room sofa; then one night, as I opened the street door, I heard voices in the living room upstairs.

"He doesn't pay any rent, and we're crowded as it is."

"I know, I know—I'll talk to him."

I let the door click shut. As I moved up the sidewalk through the fog of green and pink and lavender colors everyone was wearing, I became aware of parties going on, of music and voices sounding in yellow windows and drifting on barbecue smoke out from blue-green backyards. I felt these counterpoints keenly, especially since Marguerite and I had just become lovers, and I thought she could have argued for at least thirty seconds on my behalf. At the theater, I bought a ticket and went in.

"Stuart."

For a second all I could see was blue light and faces like half moons, but then a hand waved. It was Sasha, who patted the seat beside her. After *Bringing Up Baby*, we walked around the loop of gingerbread cottages, and I told her what had happened.

"Oh, big deal. You can sleep with me—on the floor."

We looked at each other, our faces visible by the light filtering through leaves, and I felt the understanding change between us. She smiled out from under the brim of her baseball cap, its tiny bells clicking in the breeze. We had met while cleaning house—we worked for the same woman—and our status as summer bohemians without trust funds had made us allies early on. As we sustained this easy, mutual gaze in the darkness and ocean wind, however, I wondered if something more intimate were not implied. We had reached her house.

"Sshh—they're asleep . . ."

Under a street lamp on the corner sat a yellow house so delicate it might have contained dolls rather than college girls. She lifted the garage door to reveal a privacy screen of horizontal bamboo slats. Behind this she bent into the darkness, striking a match. The candle lit, an impromptu apartment of bed, dresser, and photographs hovered in the shadows.

We undressed, and though it was all innocent, we still both looked, a couple of times. I had unrolled her sleeping bag on the cement beside her queen-size mattress, and from down there the sight of the concupiscent little minx sitting up in a sleeveless undershirt and gathering up her hair—of her breasts, lips, and curls all underlit by the candle on the bedstand—was enough to make me pray for blindness. Because it sure looked like that had been my mistake with Marguerite, and I wasn't wild about getting kicked out again.

"'Night," she said—like a sister. She puffed out the candle, and the scenery outside shone like cold, blue milk.

"'Night," I said, and fell wide awake, on guard against snores, farts, and erections, while she drifted and was soon asleep.

The move to Sasha's garage resolved so many problems, put out so many brushfires, that the next morning when I returned to Marguerite's apartment for my bike and duffle bag, we wound up going out for coffee. Now that things were over between us, we got along great. I wanted to hit the beach.

"Oh, come on, Stuart," Marguerite said. "Wait a little longer. You have to meet him. You two have so much in common."

She was always showing off her new friends like rings, but when the guy finally did show up a half hour later, I felt by her lush effusion that she was already sleeping with him. The guy was a tall, ethereal drifter from Manhattan whose name sounded like "Junghans Wier." After shaking my hand, he sprawled in his chair and began to look around as if he might enjoy himself more at another table. He swung his heavy black hair behind his shoulders.

"He's an artist," Marguerite kept telling me, "and he's going to have a show in Edgartown."

Without exactly twirling my index finger, I sat and listened while Marguerite prompted him with effervescent questions, though she needn't have. As if on cue—now that we were quiet—Junghans began with ineffable hauteur to tell us everything we didn't ask: about himself, his art, and his vision, so suavely passing off his impressions as received critical opinion that you would think he were already some kind of cultural monument, and displaying for everyone in the coffee shop the sort of convex narcissism that passes for profundity on the larger island. He was unemployed, poor thing. Why? Because he had just turned down a job at *Life* magazine because some beast there asked him to ponytail his hair, and faced with that oppression, he fled to the Vineyard to find his vision. Well, as a guy cleaning bathrooms, it was all I could do to push back my chair without knocking it over and to say goodbye without hawking up an oyster. But I did say it, and politely. He didn't respond; he was ponytailing his hair.

By the time I had biked into Edgartown, I was in such a rage that on impulse I ran the bike up to the porch and went inside the offices of the *Vineyard Gazette*.

"Okay," the woman said. "Let me read this back to you:

'Marvelous Man: six-foot-four, blond and tan, magnificently collected strength to do the desirable deed. Teaching, trenching, tutoring, cleaning. You name it. Call Stuart Goodpasture.'"

The two other women in the office turned in their chairs with visible astonishment.

"You can't run that," said one of them.

"Why not?" said the first woman. "Housework, right? It ought to get some attention."

"What's trenching?" asked the third woman.

"Oh," I said, blasé, "post holes, ditches."

For weeks I had been reading housecleaning ads by college students who seemed to be wilting of anemia, but now I would really get ahead. Now I was set. Over a celebratory cup of coffee in Edgartown, I watched all the people who seemed to own the world walking by: crowds of stunning blondicity—everywhere blonds with prancing ponytails. And then with the sunshine of late afternoon in my eyes, I biked out to my only cleaning gig, the only money I made that would put me on a par with the elegant Mr. Junghans—a young couple, arrivistes, whose new house was so sparkling that I scarcely knew where to clean. I hadn't set my bike on the grass when Jean came out the screen door, down the stairs.

"Stuart, could I have a word with you please? Gary and I think you do a wonderful job, but he noticed that you didn't clean behind the toilet last week. In the guest room?"

I was stunned; I thought I was the only one who knew that.

"He can be very demanding, I'm afraid," Jean said.

The white legs of Gary appeared in the screen door. "Come on, Jean. I don't see anything happening in the kitchen yet."

"Company." She touched my shoulder. "We might invest in a movie."

"I'm sure he's fascinated." Gary held the door and I followed. He reminded me of my father's old business partners, back-slapping, amoral, and mediocre men whose only claim to notice was the ostentation of their houses, cars, and wives. Our eyes met—long enough to discuss and close the subject of our bonding. I had been hired to clean his house, after all, not sit and chat with his wife. He let go and I caught the screen door inches from my face.

"So you gotta be outta here in forty-five minutes," he was telling me. "Where do you live anyway? I told her to call you—"

"I did call, Gary, but those girls didn't know where to find him."

"Can we please get something going in here? Jesus Christ, this is important to me! I don't want to have to order out at the last minute like last time—"

"I am, Gary. I'm doing the best I can . . . "

I went upstairs while they played George and Martha, and started vacuuming the throw rugs, sucking them into the nozzle, then splashed Lysol all over the guest bathroom like it was some sexy patchouli. It just really annoyed me that Marguerite was screwing that phony Junghans who was going to have a show in Edgartown. An artist—well, I'm a Janitorial Artist, and toilet bowls are my medium. And when the guilty party stared up at me, I made my statement by passing it over again, and the critics raved over the ambiguity of intentionality.

For the space of the next week, until my ad came out in the weekly paper, the days poured fluently into a bath of warm color and high summer haze. Since her roomates were gone, Sasha and I played tennis with their rackets. We biked to the beaches. We jumped off that bridge to Edgartown. Bright turquoise silence of sand dunes, privacy, and nude swimming, of holding paperback pages against the Atlantic wind, all fell slowly into long, cool evenings; and on our way home, Sasha and I would stop at the Silk Purse for happy hour to plump a free dinner of the chicken wings and listen to an herbal balladeer sing his plaints of love. Full and quite peaceful, we then sprawled over the wicker chairs on the little front porch of the doll house. On the asphalt courts across the street, guys were sweating out basketball games; and, watching a boy and girl bopping tennis balls in the loud twilight, we talked in a desultory way of what we wanted from life.

"Kids. Nice job. Nice house," she would say. "How about you? Where would you like to be?"

"Beyond irony," I said one night.

"Oh, God," she said, "tell me about it. I'm sick of housework. You wouldn't believe how many shirts that guy owns."

We floated on the misunderstanding until she spoke into my thoughts. "I'd love to come back every summer. Forever. Happily ever after."

I knew what she meant. The atmosphere of peace had become almost narcotic in effect, and I began to see why this had been my father's island of refuge during his marriage and why my mother had been so enraged a month earlier when I told her that I was coming here. It was an old refrain, one that my father gave me when I called him for money and one that my mother played on her blues harmonica: a year out of college with no direction, she screamed; I was becoming a dilettante. Well, I thought, so what? What's your point? At least I was helping Sasha fend off guys, and a few backed out of the garage when I spoke up out of the darkness. And, besides, I decided to try and write an article for the weekly gazette. That was a direction.

"Spiritual perfection wouldn't be bad," I said.

"Oh, did I tell you I'm reading *Franny and Zooey?*" she said.

I had begun to explore the island, taking the bike path out toward Chilmark, which was rumored to be the home of famous authors and which then took shape in my mind as the island's seat of kings. But I never got farther than a certain field I found one day, where I stopped my bicycle between two tall elms. The shadow of a cloud would roll with a rising and falling hiss of ocean wind across its grass—a place of beechen green and shadows numberless where the hues of grass flowed in unseen waves of wind back under the willows and around the grazing sheep. They were all one, the beaches, wealth, celebrities, and a pasture like this—all one, indissoluble elements of the wind and lavender hours of dusk, the privilege we felt under these stars—huge, cloudy symbols of a high romance. I was always reluctant to leave, but I would not blunder into the meadow physically. And so I looked instead for the barefoot boy sitting in a tree, swinging his legs or poised in some frustrated kiss with an eternal girl, lips never touching but always knowing what it is to want. He wasn't there, of course, but I was pleased that I could envy him.

"Ronda, Rhoda—this is Stuart Goodpasture. Stuart—"

The two sisters—Sasha's housemates—were not too thrilled on their return from Boston, to find a man living with them. And while it would be unfair to blame them, for weeks I could trace the decline of the summer to their arrival; their bickering and disappointment pressurized the small rooms, as they holed up in their bedroom, whispering, then came downstairs to ignore me.

"That's a nice guitar in your room," I said. "You play?"

Rhoda, an enormous blond whose feet were larger than mine, shifted her shoulders around at the fridge and said, "You been using my salad dressing?" Her sister sprang through the door and said she hadn't touched it.

"I could teach you some chords," I said.

"I really don't have the time."

"Oh, it's easy," I said. "Won't take you five minutes."

She turned and under the bare yellow bulb her face was hard with the anger of an unpopular party girl. "What I'm trying to say, Stuart, is that I don't like people touching my stuff, so I don't want you or anyone else touching my guitar!"

"But I could teach you to play!"

"I said, 'No,' Stuart!"

The screen door smacked like a slap, and her sister bounced back inside with a bundle of tennis rackets under her arm. She was a tough but shapely brunette who knew she was popular.

"Hey, you play tennis . . . " I said, cheerfully.

"You can't borrow my racket," little Ronda said. She sprang up the stairs, with all five rackets, and closed the door to her room.

The sisters' return to the doll house put the kibosh on the life Sasha and I had enjoyed, there amid the lush ocean trees and the twilight of tennis on the public courts. The connection may have been coincidental, but as they filled the nights with a medley of slamming doors and yelling at each other from one end of the house to the other, Sasha stopped coming home, and I felt abandoned.

One night, though, I persuaded her to ride with me to my strange and lovely meadow, and the evening bloomed into a twilight of dying brilliance over the grass, creek, and willows. And all I wanted was to kiss her lips, take her hands, and walk back among the shadows, where we could lie together in the gathering dark.

"Sublime," I said.

"Yeah," she said; "it's really cute."

I followed on my bike, taking last looks until we entered the woods. Sasha's ballcap with the tiny bells was clicking, and I followed their chimes through the darkening world. And though I knew it to be irrational, when everything came apart after that night, I always thought back to that one dumb moment between us.

"For you," the blond said, as I came inside. "Phone!" The receiver waved at me from the stairwell.

"I'm calling long distance," a man said. "Is this the Marvellous Man? Oh, good. Let me give you my number."

My ad—it came out that day. I wrote his number on a slip of paper.

"Wonderful. I'm calling on the behalf of a very important Broadway producer who is renting a house in Chilmark for the month of August? And we need someone to clean."

His voice was soft and sibilant.

"Well, there are a few particulars to cover first, though. I know this man; he's very picky. First, you would have to clean every day, six days a week, for several hours. And he throws lots of parties. Can you help throw a party?"

Maybe.

"Great. Wonderful. And you could spend the night."

Why would I do that?

"Well, of course," he said. "I mean you do want to make some money this summer, don't you?"

It took a second. "It's out of the question. Can't do it."

"Can't? What do you mean, can't?"

"My girlfriend would object," I said. "We're engaged. We'll be married in August, and besides, I'm not—"

"Girlfriend? Engaged?" His voice went up. "What is this shit? Is that ad for real or what?"

"I don't know what you mean by 'for real,' Jack, but it was on the up and up. Teaching, tutoring, cleaning, yard work—"

"Then what the hell is 'trenching'?"

"Digging ditches, post holes—"

"You fucking little cockteaser!" And the wham-slam of the receiver emphasized his point long distance.

I had never anticipated that kind of reaction, and my disquiet made me rather awkward the next morning when I talked to the managing editor of the *Gazette*. Since the day I placed my first ad, I had been hounding the guy for a chance to contribute, and on this day he finally sent me down the street to cover an exhibit of scenic photographs. When I returned to his office with my article, the sunlight of 4:00 P.M. threw a slash of green brilliance across his desk blotter while he

slashed with red pencil through my pages of copy. You know how an-
noying it was to have to review Junghans' photographs? I mean, how
many times have you seen sand dunes, sunken snow fences, eel grass,
and gulls? The bad part was that it was a great show, and the worst
part was that I said so in print. The editor slung my copy in a wire
basket. "I'll see if we can fit it in."

Without exactly coasting on my laurels, I then hit Edgartown for a
celebratory cup of coffee, and whom do I see but Marguerite and Junghans talking to two other people, and when I crossed the street to say
"hello," they all got into a jeep and roared down the street. I couldn't
believe it; she even waved at me. And all I wanted to do was tell Junghans that I liked his pictures. Then, as I stood there, it dawned on me
who the two other people were: James Taylor and Carly Simon.

The rest of the afternoon went straight uphill, when Gary fired me.
You know how some guys have no sense of humor? Well, he's one of
them, and first I was late, and then he caught me chit-chatting with
Jean in the kitchen.

"Stuart!" She called out, as I rolled in. Her mouth was all tugged
down, hooked with fishing weights of concern. "Gary and I think you
do a wonderful job, and we would never complain, but Gary says you
didn't mop behind the refrigerator last week."

I couldn't believe where this guy was willing to look, just to give
me a hard time.

"And I only mention this because he's going sailing next week and
I'll be alone for a week by myself, here—"

Gary's pale arms appeared in the screen door, fists at his belt. "Do
you want to get those beers or shall I? There's none in the door."

"Did you try the third shelf? Well, try the third shelf. Behind the
egg salad." We went inside. "This movie thing. Oh!" And she swatted
her hand as if at mosquitoes. "Did I tell you we're trying to have a
baby?"

It was an hour later; the cleaning was done, and we were sipping
iced tea in the kitchen. Gary and his pink-shirted pals were mumbling
on the deck. "He really wants a son." She watched him. "And I think
this'll change him, I really do."

"Five minutes," I told her.

She tried the pasta again, lowering a long green noodle into her
mouth. "Oh, hell," she said. "This noodle is limp."

"I hate it when you say that."

We laughed, our bodies close, hers up against mine.

"What's all this?"

Gary stood in the door, his face the color of boneless ham.

She pushed past me. "Ham salad's in the meat bin," she called, and touched the corner of her eye, as if to adjust her contact lens or wipe away a tear, and went upstairs to her room.

If Gary hadn't come in I might have kissed her; I should have done it anyway. He didn't love her; she was his maid, and I did the cleaning. I hated him but I did not fear him. And these thoughts had me in the clouds a few moments later as I lifted my bike off the grass. The screen door banged. One foot was on the ground, the bike aslant between my legs.

"Stuart?" Gary was walking toward me, his feet broad and powerful in Roman sandals. "Sorry, it's just not working out."

He shook my hand and left behind a five dollar bill. He wrapped his forearms into a massive display of muscles and hair across his heavy chest. The macho man in a pink shirt and lemon shorts. But he'd won. And hadn't Jean treated me like a little brother, after all? I wiped my hand on my jeans.

The screen door clacked. It was Jean on the front porch, and when she crossed her arms beneath her breasts, I realized they had discussed this. She might have said anything on my behalf, but it was nothing that came to mind for all of us. We formed a triangle of silence and intention, and then it was over.

But it wasn't over, not yet. When I got back to the doll house, the bad karma was flaring up from Ronda and Rhoda, who were doing their sister thing in the kitchen. They were cutting tiny labels and taping them onto their items of food, and as I stepped through the electric stillness to get a can of my beer, feeling as if I were crossing a trip wire, they wouldn't look at me.

"No one's accusing anyone," tough little Ronda went on. "Alls I'm saying is that I bought butter and now it's gone."

"And it's not like we can afford to feed everyone." Big Rhoda drew a magic marker around a bottle of French dressing.

As I opened my beer, the stick of butter that Rhoda put back in the fridge spoke to me: "This butter is not community property, so hands off!" it read.

"Don't look at me," I said. "I'm not eating your junk."

"You don't even live here."

"You don't pay any rent."

"And we're already crowded enough as it is."

"I told you he's my guest," Sasha said. "And he's in the garage, so he's not even hurting you!"

The brunette turned in a rage. "Alls I'm saying is I don't want no one ever touching my stuff ever again. Is that clear? Not even you. I mean it."

The enormous blond lumbered around to face her. "I told you it was only one cup of brown rice. I don't know about the spaghetti."

"Get your own fucking brown rice. What am I, made of money?"

"Sugar and spice and everything nice," I said.

"Excuse me, Stuart," the big blond said. "Fuck you."

We were all having a bad day, which I discovered when I glanced at her thigh, where a bruise was spreading. "How'd you get that? Some guy touch you with a ten-foot pole?"

The brunette looked at me, sharp like a wolverine. "Hey, Stuart, go fuck yourself ten times hard up the asshole with a chain saw."

"Hey, come on, you two. You've just had too much caffeine today."

Sasha bolted out the screen door, smacking it behind her. Now I had really done it—kicked out by Marguerite, fired by Jean, and now I'd ruined her rooming arrangement and didn't have enough money to leave the island. By the time I got outside, to the outdoor shower rigged to the tree, she was at the end of the block, and I wasn't sure whether I was chasing her to apologize or simply running from the sisters.

The streets were cool and growing dark; the green of the trees was the color of night, and when she went round the corner beneath a street lamp, she vanished. Once or twice I thought I could hear the clicking of little bells, but the streets were empty. As I walked around the circle of cottages that night, all I heard was fights, as though some contagion of disappointment had filled the island of paradise, all those voices shouting disenchantment into the windy darkness—loans, mortgages, custody, a great load of misery coated with sugar.

"I'm sorry," Sasha said.

"Maybe I should move out."

Her silhouette had finally appeared against distant lights, there beneath the dome of the bandstand, and she was alone on the wooden bench, a little hunched and looking down. Now she stood so close in the summer dark that I felt the pressure between us; in spite of all the other young people around us, we always came back to each other. And I realized that I was in love with her, that I had been looking for Sasha in all those other encounters.

"I want you to stay, Stuart." Her voice gentle. "I like you." And we walked all the way home to our garage with nothing to say beyond the light clasp of our fingers. She puffed out the candle. The night scenery shone a hot blue.

"You know, Stuart, you don't have to sleep on the floor."

And I knew that I would never leave her, that I had found in Sasha the other half of my soul, so Junghans and Marguerite could have each other. I even blessed them as I climbed up on my elbows and got in beside Sasha; for, in finding her, I had found myself.

Brightness. Wind slapping against . . . something. The cotton blanket was off me. Anyone walking by could have seen me lying naked on the bed. In a few moments, I was in my boxers at the kitchen door. Latched from inside. Cupping my hands around my face, I got my reflection. Out front, the wicker furniture was all taken in, the door locked. Shades down. A tennis ball was whopping the practice wall. The courts empty. No one on the sidewalks. Leaves roaring with ocean wind. The cool of the morning felt like September. Beneath the shower head rigged to the oak tree and behind the blue plastic curtain, I soaped up, then biked into Edgartown.

"Okay," she said—the woman in the *Gazette* office. "Let me read this back to you."

The other two women swivelled around to listen.

"'Mellifluous Man,'" she read. "'Girls, want to have a catty conversation about your best friend with someone who totally agrees? Call Stuart Goodpasture at . . .'"

No one was home that night, but the house was open again, so I answered the phone.

"Hi!" It was a woman. "Hi, is this the Marvellous Man? Or should I say the Mellifluous Man?"

"Sasha?" I said. "Where the hell are you?"

"We love your ads. The whole island's talking about them. Everyone wants to meet you. Wait, wait . . . someone else wants to say something."

A second woman. "Hey, is this the Marvellous Man? Hey, what's trenching? Come on, you can tell me. No, wait—"

A third woman. "Hi, Mellifluous Man? I think my best friend's a bitch, don't you agree?"

"Marguerite?" I said. "Jean? Is that you? Sasha?"

Laughter at the other end; many women in a room. Five married women having a party because their husbands had gone sailing for a week. One woman began to monopolize the line. She asked if I had herpes and liked jazz. Then spoke in a hush. "Go to a literary function tomorrow night." Then loudly said, "Okay, 'bye now, Marvellous Man." And hung up.

And so the next night, I found myself walking through the summery twilight of a country road. In the Oak Bluffs library that afternoon, I had scanned the *Gazette* and found an ad for a poetry reading in Chilmark, so I was headed there, at last. Before I left the house, though, the sisters returned with some big guy friends, and told me that Sasha had gone to Boston for a week, so I was welcome to get out while she was gone, and, if I didn't, they would call the police and have me thrown out. At Marguerite's, no one had seen her in a week; she was now living with Junghans, who was house-sitting in some grand place down by Lucy Vincent beach. And yet if they were all having such a great time, my own great time wasn't far behind—or at least that's what I believed, which inspired me along that country road through nowheresville.

Dusk. Fireflies. Cicadas. A farmhouse among the trees, its white paint glowing with a porch lamp that shone against the spread of darkness and the still-luminous evening sky. Then with a shout, I did know where I was, and I ran down between the two big elms into my pasture. Not since my disquieting visit with Sasha had I been there, and now it felt like I was home at last with something real, the reason I had remained. The meadow was still. The air above the creek was chilling into vapors of mist; sheep trotted away into the dark as I approached, crossing the meadow at last.

My foot slipped in a soft pad of something foul, and as I swung my hands for balance, I felt all my twenty-two years crash beside me like a grand piano. I seemed to catapult up out of the noise straight into the air. And when I landed on the branch of that tree, I found myself looking down and saw below me, and looking up at me, a bewildered young man in white clothes and wet sneakers. He stood in mist and manure. His life was half over; he had accomplished nothing, done nothing, aspired so far to even less—to relaxing. He might die any day —hit by a car while biking around the island—and come to nothing.

I looked down at my shit-smeared tennis sneakers, then up again, and there on the branch, bright against the darkness, swinging my legs, sat Stuart, sarcastically pleased by all my failure and confusion. He smiled at me and I glowered at him. The sensation of seeing me up there caused an irrational fear I'd never felt before—afraid for my life but aware of my stupidity as I vaulted the rail fence and waved at the low beams coming on in the fog.

The stone church by the pond sat, windows glowing, in the deepening dusk; as I paid my two dollars at the screen door and walked to the back row, I shook off the nerves by imagining an audience of foxes and hens in velvet jackets and bonnets.

"Before we begin," said the poet, "I'd like to introduce a dear, dear friend of mine who founded the most beautiful paper in the world, the *Vineyard Gazette*. Everyone, please—Henry Walker Hadley."

We all leaned upward. An elderly man in the front pew stood. Searsucker jacket, yellow bow tie, and pinkish glasses—he acknowledged our applause with a nod of his head.

"Thank you," the poet said.

It was a Unitarian church, so there were no religious icons—just the poet, a fabulous blond, wife of the island's preeminent author and queen of its social life. Was she my caller?

"I just want to thank you all for coming here tonight. It gives me such faith in myself, faith in all of us, and I know Lee will be glad to hear about it. I would like to begin tonight with my Paris poems. I think of all the world there are only two places I love the most, and they are Paris and Martha's Vineyard. This particular poem was written on the balcony of some very dear friends of ours who live in Paris. We were having cocktails on their balcony one beautiful night last spring and looking at the City of Lights, and I just found myself thinking how fortunate Lee and I are to share the beauty of Paris and Martha's Vineyard. So here it is. It's called 'Paris, June 25th, 1982.'"

Sitting on your Paris balcony one night in June
Cocktails in hand
I cannot help but think how beautiful
Is the City of Lights
In the world without exception
But for one
That tiny isle in New England—
Little Martha's Vineyard.

Lulled by the sense of tranquility recollected with emotion, I drifted off, then sat up to applause. Everyone was clapping.

"There you are!" An enormous three-hundred-pound woman was lumbering, knock-kneed toward me, pushing the folding chairs aside. "You made it!"

I turned back around and saw another woman coming right at me. Both were accelerating and extending their arms. I stepped back, and they crashed in an embrace. Among the devotees surrounding the poet, a tall woman with curls was waiting to have her book signed. She looked at me. I went closer. Then she gave me a go-thither look. So I plopped into the second pew. Someone swept by and sat in front of me—a pretty young woman, her thick blond hair, all ash and browngold, wrapped in a French twist.

"Nice reading," she said.

"Yeah. Very good. Did you enjoy it?"

A lovely, intelligent smile. "Yes, very much. Did you?"

"Well, it was okay."

We looked away, then at each other again.

Her voice became confidential. "I really didn't think it was that good," she said.

"Yeah, I wasn't too wild about it either."

"Actually," she said, "I thought it kind of sucked."

"Yeah, I hated it."

Then we beamed at each other. Green and golden eyes.

"So . . . " She was confident, friendly.

"You know, you sound familiar. Have we met before?"

The smile gone. "Me? Impossible. I never spoke to you on the phone—"

"Izzy—!" A tall man in summer whites. "Izzy? What a surprise. I'm so glad you decided to come. Didn't you get my message?"

And that was it. The next thing I knew, they were locking up the church, and I was on the road, hitchhiking. Izzy zoomed by in a sports car. She gave me a look of apology over the steering wheel. The pretender, seated beside her, was still talking.

A station wagon pulled over and I jumped in back, with an urge to say "Follow that car!" Then, to my astonishment, I saw who my saviors were. Henry Walker Hadley and his wife, driving. The sports car vanished into a red blur of taillights.

"Wonderful reading," I said.

Neither wife nor husband answered.

"So," I said, "her husband is the guy who wrote *The French Lieutenant's Sophie*? Great book."

"Well, do you know who this is?" Mrs. Hadley turned her head in profile. "This," she said, "is Henry Walker Hadley," and rolled out her heavy-ringed hand in a flourish.

"No kidding. Hey, nice to meet you. That's a handsome newspaper."

They rode in silence. I kept talking—all about my art review and how the editor refused to pay me for it.

Mr. and Mrs. Hadley looked at each other.

"What did you say your name was again, dear?"

I told her.

"And where are you from? Ah, yes, Princeton's a lovely town. We have some wonderful friends there. Do you possibly know the Urbanks?"

I did, indeed. Their son, who was my age, was a lacrosse-stick-wielding, gang-raping, sadistic pig who went to Dartmouth.

"Oh, we're great friends," I said.

"How's this?"

Edgartown. Crowds of beautiful people were crossing our headlights in a pastel mist as Old Henry said good-night. I felt sorry for him, suddenly; he sounded alone. But I never saw him again nor, for that matter, Jean or Gary. Years later, though, I did have dinner with Henry's strange and lovely niece.

The streets were hectic, but I hoped to spot Izzy's sports car. And this night was the whole summer. The universal party was rising on the bell curve of high summer, sidewalks surging and cars cruising, everyone going somewhere faster, brighter. At the Silk Purse, bouncers were coralling people inside; once I was inside, someone pulled on my sleeve from the table behind me.

"Have you seen Junghans?"

It was Marguerite. "He was supposed to meet me here an hour ago. Shit." She looked across the crowded bar. "We're supposed to go to James and Carly's tonight. You don't have a car, do you? Fuck, I knew this would happen. And now it's like I'm so worried about them. Why? Oh, God, Stuart, I thought everyone knew . . . their marriage is in real trouble."

Something dark was thrown over my face from behind, and what I grabbed was a handful of felt ball cap with clicking bells. It was Sasha, hilariously drunk. Where had she been? Come on, come on—party on the beach. We were in someone's jeep, grasping the roll bar, my hand keeping her ball cap on my head. At the beach there were cars and jeeps. People ran across the sand under the summer moon. Sasha had to tell me something. She waited until we were alone. She patted the car—stand here, by her.

"My God, Sasha, where were you? When did you get back from Boston?"

"I'm so happy— I have to tell you—" Laughing drunkenly, she put her hand on my chest. "Am I being too dumb or is this all obvious to you?"

"Where have you been? I missed you so much. The sisters . . . "

Some guy shouted, "Hey, they nuked Boston!"

And there on the horizon a burst of blue light was blazing high up into a vast dome over the surface of the water. Everyone began shouting that Boston had been nuked, their faces half-moons in the eerie semi-dark. Sasha took my hand as we looked at the explosion, and I knew again she was my best, my real chance. The nuclear blast was mushrooming over the ocean.

"We have such wonderful conversations. I can tell him anything," she was saying. "And he loves Salinger."

We looked at each other across three feet of electric blue light, and I said, "Sasha—I love Salinger." It took a second.

She waved at someone. "How about breakfast tomorrow? What? Are you pissed off or something?"

I couldn't get my mind around it. "Sasha . . . I was hoping, stupid as it sounds, that you were talking about me."

She didn't laugh right away, then apologized when she did. She got playful. She really didn't want to have anything to do with me, either.

"You lost your hat! Come on, now, don't be a poop!" And tugged her ball cap down over my eyes, to my ears.

"Electrical line," some guy shouted. He cupped his hands, shouting at everyone on the beach. "Car accident. Hit a power box. Lights out all down the beach."

They made a wild party down on the beach, and from the grassy dune where I sat beside a half-sunken snow fence, amid the ocean wind of surf and gulls, everyone's voices roared with the clicking of Sasha's tiny bells beside my ears. They cheered the car accident as they cheered the arrival of more people and ice chests of beer, the privilege of being together here and now. I sat there brooding until love and fame had sunk to nothingness, then caught a ride home with someone too drunk to drive.

A northern wind was boxing the loose-latched shutters of the *Gazette*'s little house early next morning. I left my ad with the girl behind the Dutch door. The offices were empty and quiet.

"'Moribund Man.'" She looked at me, confused. "That's it? Just your name?"

"That's all."

"Okay. Do you want to pay cash or you want us to bill you?"

"The editor has my address," I said. "He'll know what to do with it." She looked confused. "He told me they don't pay freelancers—after I spent a whole day writing the article. Actually, he screamed at me over the phone. Why? What?"

"We're not supposed to say." Leaning over the door, she glanced into the empty newsroom. "He disappeared again last night. Last time they say he was gone for six months, and they found him drunk in Jacksonville."

As I came toward the Edgartown coffee shop, I was unable to disentangle the image of two people outside its doors. That was Sasha, but I didn't know the man who sat on the railing above her, swinging his legs with a look of sarcastic pleasure on his face. As his gaze met mine, I remembered the tree of last night, the ghost in the branches, with a chill.

"Didn't recognize you with a haircut."

She smiled up at him, and the ironic smirk left his face.

"It's so goddamn hot," Junghans said, and we didn't bother to shake hands. She had made her decision, fine—I almost laughed. Silly to become bitter, and besides, now that I was leaving, we got along great—so well, in fact, that I even gave Junghans a lead on a job, a piece of paper with a phone number I'd found in my pockets while packing. "He's a Broadway producer?" he said. "He wants to throw parties? And I can live there?" His look said "Wow," and you could see him calculate his future. The waitress flirted with us.

"Don't they look like brothers?" she said.

And as Junghans and I regarded each other rather coolly, it was impossible to say which of us felt more insulted. I hitched a ride to the ferry, then stood under a coffee shop TV, amazed—my friend Jack in a local commercial.

When the stores and people of Vineyard Haven had diffused into the glittering haze, I stuffed my *Gazette* into the barrel and leaned on the ship's railing along with everyone else. The bright sea was churning astern. We were a common crowd, backpackers with bicycles, brushing hair against the turquoise, chiming wind and looking where we'd been—a lump on the broad back of the ocean. And when I thought of the boy in the tree, I leaned on my elbows and spat into the ocean; he had vanished along with the pleasure of being young, of fooling around. He was back there on the island, beneath the concave ceiling of sky.

The time had come to work. On the phone my mother had asked me to come home, but I wouldn't. And when I called my sister to tell her my plans, I learned that she had not yet heard from our father, who had told me that he would call and tell her about the divorce himself. My family, like the island, were behind me now. We had another half hour yet, so I went forward, alone, to watch the mainland rising.

|||||||| I Wish You Wouldn't Be That Way

WHEN THE PHONE CALL CAME, IT WAS LATE IN THE AFTER-noon, and Moriah Goodpasture was only two weeks away from taking the bar exam, the summer after her last year in law school.

"Hello, dear, this is your old man calling. Just wanted to say hello and be sure everything is fine. Are you all set for money? Do you need any?"

"Dad, where are you?"

"Right now, darling?"

That winter, as the divorce between her parents moved in from the horizon to plant itself as large, square, and solid as a house in their lives, her father had become hard to find. It was as if the more real the divorce became, the more elusive he was in response, until no one knew where he was, much less who he was. He was said to be in Jacksonville, Florida—his home town—but in the last two weeks her brothers Brian and Jay had called to tell her something else about him. But she wanted to hear it from him herself.

"Yeah, right now," Moriah said, pouring herself a second cup of coffee, amid the open case books and outlines. "What did you think I was talking about? The future?"

"Well, I'm traveling, dear."

"So, did you get a lawyer when you were down there? Brian and Jay said you went to Jacksonville to sue the bank for ruining the trust funds. Did you hire a lawyer yet?"

"It's not that simple, dear."

"Why not? All you have to do is sue the trustee for mismanaging the trust. And please stop calling me 'dear.' I'm not your little girl anymore."

"I'm not in Jacksonville, honey."

"What difference does that make? If the trustee really sold all that land to his brother below market value, then we have a case. So?"

"I'm on my way to Oklahoma."

"Oklahoma? Why in God's name are you going to Oklahoma?"

"Then I'm going to Mexico for a while."

"*Mex*-ico? Dad, what are you talking about?"

"Honeybunch," he said. "I want you to listen carefully to what I have to tell you. Now, you know that for years now your mother and I haven't been getting along."

"I wonder whose fault that is."

"Now, honey, I wish you wouldn't be that way."

"And stop calling me 'honey.' I'm not your little girl anymore. Christ, if this is about the divorce, it's about time, Dad. Growing up at home was like living in a cross between *Who's Afraid of Virginia Woolf?* and *A Long Day's Journey into Night.*"

She waited for him to shout, but he didn't. His response caught her off guard.

"You know, you're right, dear, and I'm sorry for all the misery we caused you, and I hope one day to make it up to you—"

"Who is this?" Moriah teased, liking him against her will, for one second. "Jay, is that you?"

"Now, please, honey, let's not get sidetracked, shall we? Now, look.

Don't be angry with me, but a lot has happened to me down here. I've met someone very special who has changed my life and shown me how to love and how to accept love, which your mother could never do."

"Yeah? And what's this one's name, Tootsie? And when you met her, was she wearing tassles?" Still, he wouldn't rise to the bait, which made her cock her head sideways, quizzically.

"It's not a she, honey. It's a he."

Moriah, who had been standing, sat down, saying, "Oh, my God. Oh, my God—" She folded over her knees and came up, howling with laughter. "This is great! This is great!"

"Will you let me finish, please, dear?"

"Oh, my God! Oh, my God! Oh, my God! This is great!"

"Listen to me," he shouted, at last. "The 'he' I am talking about is the Lord, Jesus Christ. I've accepted Him into my life, and I hope you will, too, one day."

"That's disgusting," she snapped. "I don't want to hear this. I don't want to hear the sordid details of your twisted, ugly life. How dare you call and tell me this!"

"Oh, sweetheart, I wish you wouldn't be this way. I'm only trying to reach out—"

"Don't touch me!" she snapped, having forgotten this was a long-distance phone call.

He was still explaining. " . . . and I know that someday you'll mature and understand and accept my new life. After all, we are all looking for something, for a spiritual life of some kind—"

"This is disgusting," she repeated. "Who else have you told? No one, I hope. So—wait—why are you in Oklahoma?"

"Well, I'm not in Oklahoma."

"You said you were in Oklahoma."

"No. If you'd been listening, I said I was on my *way* to Oklahoma, but I'm not *in* Oklahoma."

"So, you were right and I was wrong. That still doesn't answer my question. Why are you *going* to Oklahoma?"

"Well, dear, because . . . I'm going to be married."

Moriah stood up again, in her little D.C. kitchen, and stared at the floor, which seemed to be melting away from her.

"She's a wonderful woman," her father went on. "Her name is Muriel, and I hope that one day you will love her like a mother."

"Why? Is she an alcoholic?"

"Oh, Jesus—please, Lord, heal my daughter's pain."

"Dad, if you do that again, I am going to hang up, do you hear me?"

"Well, I was hoping you would explain all this to Brian and Jay and Stuart."

"You haven't told them? You've got to be kidding."

"Well, I told Stuart. He called from the Vineyard to borrow some money, but when I told him, he hung up. And Brian hung up, and I thought Jay was with you. How is he, by the way?"

"I can't believe you're doing this. You're going to dump all your responsibility on me, aren't you? Have you even told Mom?"

Her father cleared his throat. "Well, honeybunch—"

"And stop calling me that!"

"—you know how your mother is."

"So, in other words, you didn't tell her, did you?"

"That's why I'm calling you, sweetheart. Now, tell me how you're set for money. And does Jay need any?"

"He just started working for some ridiculous industry council, so the answer is 'No.' I can't believe you're doing this to me, Dad; you are such a bastard. Why did Mom ever marry you?"

"Which brings me to another point I wanted to make, dear. Are you listening to me? Are you there?"

"And you know, the funny thing is my shrink always wants to know why, as a kid, I always wanted to grow up in another family. Well, wait'll he hears this one. I can't believe you're doing this to me! And to think there was a time when Uncle Jason might have married Mom, and he could have been my father!"

Now he got short with her. "Please try to focus! I want you to listen to me very closely now!"

Having finally scored, she relented.

"While I'm in Tulsa," he went on, "I will be working on a special project that will make us all a lot of money, and I've decided that what we ought to do is, take the money that's left in mother's trust and reinvest it, otherwise it'll just go to waste, with Bubsy and your Aunt Betty living on it. Now, while I was in Jacksonville, I looked into having the power of attorney switched, and since you will soon be a lawyer and could do all this work gratis. Are you listening to me? The geologists' report says it's dry, but Jesus has shown Muriel the way to other oilwells—"

"You weasel," she said. "You pull this slimy stuff, running away with another woman, and you want me to talk about reinvesting our inheritance with a bunch of religious lunatics? You're disgusting! You are such a slime bag! I wish to God that you weren't my father. I wish I had another father. I wish to God that I was someone else and that we'd never met, you depraved, psychopathic—"

"Now, dear, I wish you wouldn't be like that. Please, hear me out on this. This call is costing me plenty, as it is—"

"Oh, really?" Moriah said. "Well, I have just one question for you, then, Dad."

"Yes, dear. What's that?"

"Tell me if it sounds like I'm hanging up!"

And she did. Twice.

||||||| Wingtips

AFTER LUNCH ONE THURSDAY AFTERNOON NOT VERY LONG ago, I found myself loitering in the summer heat at the windows of Massey's shoe store on 18th Street. Wingtips—a pair gleamed on a brass pedestal behind the glass. The bells chimed and a man came out in the sunshine. Brushed silver hair, yellow power tie, and Brooks Brothers suit—so distinguished he might have been an ambassador. On his feet were new wingtips, which caught the sun and flashed. He seemed to shine all over. And yet, he looked a little silly holding that plastic bag with his old shoes inside. In the shade of the awning, I laughed. The man glared cautiously and moved into the flow of pedestrians, no doubt feeling my smile on his back.

For until then life for me in Washington, D.C., had flowed along rather pleasantly. I didn't walk the shadowed valleys, but then again I didn't exactly achieve the sunlit summits either in a city where power glittered on inaccessible terraces. I was a humble cottage villager who carried in his rucksack daydreams of effortless and precocious success, and I was still trying then to make that quantum leap onto the staff of a senator. Shooting for speech writer or communications director. The trade council I worked for, though, the A.S.C.C., was nothing to sneer at. We represented hundreds of millions in sales, here and abroad. And we had a humongous trade show coming up in September, when I would play spokesman to the national media. No, the A.S.C.C. wasn't missiles, perhaps, but then again we weren't butter, either.

As I crossed Dupont Circle on my way back up Connecticut Avenue, bums shook plastic cups and dry voices asked for my spare change. You see them every day until they vanish into the green shade, and they were far away that day because I was flashing back to a scene, my last seizure to own a specific kind of shoe.

"Mom . . . " An autumn morning in the fifth grade. "They're not Beatle boots; they're galoshes!"

"You straighten up, mister, right this second, do you hear me? If you miss that bus you are going to walk to school!"

"Everybody'll laugh! They'll call me a nimrod; they'll call me a square!"

I had reached my office building by now, and stepping into the elevator allowed the doors to shut the memory out.

The afternoon waned but I got nothing done. Shadows of the Venetian blinds drooped over my computer screen and bled down my white shirt, and I was alive to the blaze of summer outside and the cool dark of corkboard inside. There was a press release I should have written that day but didn't. Bowing a rubber band, I fired a paperclip and stung the slats. Creating the council's image was no small task, however. I fired again. The beady red phone light had been blinking for a few moments when Joy paged me. "Jay Goodpasture, call on line six, Jay Goodpasture—"

"The release?" I said, to Larry. "Fine. Tomorrow. Why?"

Larry Drapers was my boss and the A.S.C.C.'s director, an anxious and ineffectual man who fell back on maternal silence to inflict guilt. The line went quiet. But I had been flacking for a year now, so trying to appeal to my conscience was a wrong step. It was professional to feel little guilt over anything that didn't touch you personally, which included my job.

"We have that big press conference in a week," he went on, in the authoritative tone. "I want to see those press packets on Monday. And I am not kidding. Do you hear me? Are you there?"

That was my job as wordsmith, to spin golden threads of syntax into bales of verbal straw: releases, newsletters, and brochures. But that was life at a trade council. The *Post* might be rife with stories about bombings or wars or grand mal seizures of the stock market, but all I ever did was trolley along in that cute shuttle train between senate buildings. Or listen to Larry.

"You got it," I kept telling him. "Snax-Po—historic event, no sweat. I'll do it first thing tomorrow morning, okay? Jesus."

I raised the blinds on the construction site across the street. On the reticulated skeletal frame, men in hard hats were ascending and descending stairs in another unfinished project rising in steel against the sun, a city glassed in dreams. And when the warm hours began their heavy descent in the stillness of my workspace, I lowered my face onto my folded arms and came up again outside on the mall. We had been playing softball when I leaped for an outfield catch, kept rising, soaring into the sun, and my legs went down, and I had become a colossus bestriding the narrow mall. My softball mitt filled the sky. Shoes moving on the carpet startled me, and I awakened quickly, careful to swipe a sleeve across my cheek for the drool. The press conference lay two weeks off; I could knock out the release in the morning.

"'Night, Joy," I said. Last ones—the office was empty.

On the way down two women in the elevator were discussing a party, and as I left the building, converging with everyone else shouldering toward the Dupont station, I remembered a party from the previous weekend. Some townhouse way up Mass. Ave. Capitol Hill crowd. Great party—dancing, music, beer, people. Hawaiian shirts, tans. Motown. People on the deck, around the keg in the steel washtub of ice. Then, from out of nowhere, some Yalie with a square jaw tried to do a little social climbing on my face.

"And what do you do, Jay?" he said.

"Press secretary for an industry council," I said, and began looking around for something or someone.

"Really, which one?" He turned to three women with big hair and a visible enthusiasm for husband hunting. "We handle a lot of defense issues," he told them. "The Senator is sponsoring legislation to extend S.D.I. funding." He then looked at me.

The four of them were waiting.

"The A.S.C.C.," I said, trying to shrug my way out of this. "We do nutrition stuff mostly. Say, you know where the bathroom is?"

"The what?" asked one of the women.

"Oh, yeah." Joe Yale clicked his fingers while looking at his shoes—two-hundred-dollar casual, tassled, cordovan loafers.

I couldn't let him blurt it out, so I had to translate. "The American Snackfood and Candy Council," I said.

"That's it!" He looked up, and that smile of sudden memory became one of triumph.

"I never heard of such a thing," the second woman said, and laughed. "Oh, I'm sorry," and put a hand over her astonished mouth.

The third woman said, "Didn't I see something in the *Post* about a trade show you have coming up. What's it called again?"

"Snax-Po," I said, and they laughed as though I were telling lawyer jokes.

I laughed with them. "Hey, don't knock it," I said. "We send Tang up with the astronauts."

They thought that was a riot, but when they kept it up, I started looking around. Sometimes they get the point and lay off.

"Oh, I love this song," one of the women said.

In the living room "Baby Love" was booming—sweet and urgent and pleading—and they went surging out to dance. Someone opened the refrigerator, so I moved against the wall, and the door swung into my chest. From behind the door the party looked great—all these heads going by and all that dancing. Plenty of beautiful women, talking to other guys. The bathroom was upstairs, and at the end of the hall there was a library with a television, and the most amazing things are on cable these days—*Dark Shadows,* for one, which I hadn't seen in ages.

Anyway, as I red-lined to Takoma Park that evening after work, I had a flash. Wingtips. I began drumming the solo from "Inna Gadda Da Vida" on my thighs. Wingtips. Of course—they were perfect! I looked down at my old black penny loafers—so adolescent, so prep school. But wingtips were classics—serious shoes worn by serious men. A pair of wingtips would add throw-weight to my appearance and, therefore, my opinions. So . . . in your face, Mr. Capitol Hill smartass. And not just you but all the smarmy little shits who suck up to guys like you. I felt so high that I almost missed my station. And on impulse picked up a sixpack, then enjoyed a stroll home under leaves glazed with summer twilight.

"Goddamnit!"

As I shut the door, my sister, Moriah, was snatching newspapers and magazines off the dining room table. "I can't believe it's not here," she said. "I must have left it on the train. Shit. Fuck. Shit."

"Hey, you want to take it easy with my *Esquire?*" I slid the six into the fridge and crumpled the paper bag. "You want a Molson's? Oh, guess what—how do you like wingtips? You think they're too Reagan?"

"It's the little black one with the long strap. It's not under your coat, is it?"

"What?" I finger-snapped the bottle cap at the garbage can and missed.

"My purse, Jay. Will you please look?"

"Oh, I thought you meant a book or something. Nope, not here. You know the funny thing is I looked at them last year and said, 'God, I'm becoming just like Dad, man. No way.'"

"My wallet was in there, my credit cards, my Safeway check cashing card, my library card, my license, my Visa, my Mastercard. Goddamnit! My whole life was in that bag. I don't exist without it. I can't buy anything, I can't get money—Goddamnit, Jay, would you please get your stuff off the table? Here . . . " She thrust another book into my arms. "And not on the steps, either. I'm sorry to be such a bitch, but I'm really pissed off."

Renting a house with your sister can slow you down socially, but she was an okay housemate. She had just gotten engaged, though, and I think that was bugging her.

"Just call and cancel everything," I called downstairs.

"I will," she said, as I came back down. "But first I want to drive over to the Metro and see if anyone has turned it in."

I clicked on the TV. The network news had ended, but *Jeopardy* was on. I sank into the couch, humming the theme song, then took a long swig of the beer.

"Shit, this pisses me off. Don't let the cats out." She banged the door shut behind her.

I lifted little black Rasta into my lap, shouted, "Who was Walt Disney?" and was right for a thousand dollars.

The next morning, Friday, I sat in the sumptuous light of the window, spooning in Cheerios, drinking Coca-Cola, watching *Bullwinkle* and then *Good Morning America.* It was great to feel my childhood alive within me. My formative years, the ages one through twelve, had been filled with an indissoluble mixture of toys and television. And with the guys in my office, I shared a memory of sitcom characters and plots, from *I Love Lucy* to *The Brady Bunch,* far more than we shared any sensibility drawn from books. I don't remember even finishing a book until I got to B.U. I had escaped high school on the erudition of *Cliff's Notes.* But don't knock them—they taught me what to say in college.

That morning I drove Moriah to Dulles so she could shuttle up to Boston for her tenth reunion at Wellesley. She gave me a list of chores, including the obvious one of feeding the cats. "No, duh," I said, after she got out of the car.

"Um, Joy," I said, in the office. "If Larry asks, would you tell him that I'm up on the Hill, schmoozing? Thanks."

"Jay, he's really anxious about that press release for Snax-Po. Are the packets ready? He wants them today, if possible."

"They're fine," I said. "I'll do it Monday. No sweat."

And then I went shopping. Sweating and itching in the swampy June heat, I rambled over miles of pavement under the hot sky, ran across broad avenues, revolved through glass doors, and rose only to sink again on escalators. I made an endless circle to all of D.C.'s shoe stores for men. I was tough. I scrutinized stitching, linings, and patterns, brought shoes right up to my nose. Florsheim I compared to Johnston & Murphy in terms of price and craftsmanship. I was choosy. I strode the carpets, opened my jacket, studied my new image in mirrors. Crossing my legs, I caught a glimpse of myself. Is this how they see me? Salesmen gave up. They salaamed me on my first visit with "Hello, Sir, and how are we today?" But on my third, they said, "Hey, Frank, you wanna take this guy? I got a customer here."

My first decision was clear: to fight my mother's influence. Always,

always, always, she had bought the cheap imitation to save money. Other kids wore skin-tight Levi cords. I moped into class in Levi's factory seconds—purchased at the Lambertville flea market—with leg seams twisting across the baggy knees, looking like Emmett Kelly. On rainy days the studs hung out at the bus stop in blue-jean jackets, getting soaked and looking cool. When the bus pulled up, I would fall out of the bushes, wearing my yellow, shiny raincoat with the illustrations of Raggedy Andy on the lining, and clumsy buckle galoshes which my mother insisted were as cool as Beatle boots. But better because your feet stayed dry. "Don't be silly, Jay; do your own thing. Who cares what other people think?" But no one knocked her books to the ground or refused to sit with her in the cafeteria, and she never got into fights with popular little square jaws.

And yet, the more shoes I saw, the less decisive I became. You may not know this, but there are as many kinds of wingtips as there are industry councils. "Jesus Christ," I muttered. A few decisions were easy: color, walnut not oxblood; texture, smooth not pebble. But then there was the problem of size. Take the 11-Ds. Was there something aristocratic in the superfluous length of the toe? How could I decide? And did that mean the 10½-Ds were proletarian?

"I'm sorry," said one salesman in a cheap orange toupee, as he came swishing in with a box. "Sold the last pair of 10½-Ds in cordovan not five minutes ago. But I do have black."

A voice whispered from memory. "Black is so tacky, black is so tacky . . . " My mother—still buying my clothes! Distraught, I gazed at my thighs.

"Let me see the 11-Ds in cordovan, please."

I strutted, mashed my thumb down, desperate to locate my big toe.

"They're a little long," the salesman said. He twisted his pinky into his ear then inspected the crud that came out under the nail. "But only you can really know."

I looked down at my old penny loafers amid the tissue paper—creased with experience, as individual as a face, but just not powerful enough on a planet of office buildings.

As I went home on the red line with the box on my lap, I became sick. My angry reflection in the train windows accused me. I couldn't believe that I had bought such long and pointy shoes. I would look like a complete jerk. Worse, I would look like Bobby Rydell. When the train stopped at Union Station, I wanted to throw the box out the doors. But I began to study the shoes of other passengers. Duck-footed, pigeon-toed, scuffed, and tacky, they were a host of sad and ugly shoes without even a millimeter of unnecessary length to convey elegance. I began to examine their faces. Fat, pale, and lumpen they were—asleep, dead, and bored. They were the timeless medieval peasants whom Breughel painted dancing in the mud, people who spent their lives slogging through shadowy valleys, while I now felt the breaking warmth of sunshine across my face. We had come up into the placid evening of green suburbs, and I knew that all things come to those who dare to reinvent themselves. The windows were flashing. Outside was a lovely world.

The telephone rang. It rang again. And it was ringing in my dreams until I went stumbling between the dining room chairs, thinking: plane crash, heart attack, car accident—

"Collect call from Tony," the operator said. "Will you accept?"

"Tony? Who's Tony?"

"For Moriah, man," a deep voice said. "I got the purse."

I accepted the charges.

"She lose the purse?" the man asked.

"Uh—yeah, she lost it."

"I got it."

I sat down at the dining room table, working my eyes and mouth, and checked the clock radio—4:13 A.M. "Okay," I said. "So, now what?"

"Well, you want it back, right?"

"Yeah, yeah."

"Well, come and get it."

I wondered what time would be convenient.

"Now, man. You want the purse, come and get it now, you dig?"

I had to think a moment, but couldn't. "What do you mean? Like, now?"

"Yeah, man, now. You want the purse, right?"

I checked my wrist watch against the clock radio. I couldn't go anywhere at that hour and said so.

Silence on both ends of the line. Him breathing in my ear. Me breathing into his.

"Well," he said, "what are we going to do?"

In my position at the A.S.C.C., I had dealt with all sorts of power-ful people, from a raft of congressmen to their aides, and even a few in-tractable hair stylists. So I knew how to say "yes" and "no" and close a deal. I began to drum on my thigh.

"I got to tell you some things, though, okay? I didn't take it. I found it. So I figured, you know, like I would like it if someone did it for me, so I figure I do it for you, you dig?"

"I hear you, Tony."

"That's not my name. You got a pen?"

He told me his real name was Reginald, but every single pen I tried was dry and pencils broke.

"Nope," I said. "Wait. Nope. Hang on. Here we go. Shit. You still there? Hang on." It took us nearly ten minutes of saying everything three times to get his name, phone number, and address. And then I still had to carve impressions into an envelope with the hollow tip of a pencil.

"And when you come and get it, man, don't be bringing no police, you dig? I know there's white people and black people with bad feel-ings, but I don't want no trouble. You know, 'cause, like, I know where you live and I got your number."

"Right," I said. "Got it."

Nightmares pursued me through the sleepless hours. Turn as I might, thrusting my face into a fresh side of the pillow, my mattress would roll up on one side and send me tumbling down on the other; in doing so, it dropped me into a dark city street, where rain was drip-ping from the fire escape and glistening in puddles down the alley. Soon, I was running from a derelict movie house, with a mob of were-wolves chasing me, until the mattress rolled up the other way, and my eyes opened on the heavy bars of the blinds. With a sleepy hand, I di-aled the police. Dispatcher 210 told me not to go to Reginald or let him come to me, but Reginald wouldn't hear of it. "No, man," he said in five calls that Sunday. "You don't understand. I got a friend that's got a car. We'll drive it over there and give it to you."

"No, no, no," I said Sunday night, in the flickering dark of the tele-vision, "that's impossible . . . "

Monday morning. Larry's bald spot was waiting for me in my cubi-cle—visible on my approach—so I went to the men's room. In the third stall I found some refuge with the "Style" section. Then a pair of shoes came in and stood at the sink—Larry's seamed and cracked old Florsheim kiltie loafers—and I drew mine back from sight.

"You know," he said, toweling his hands, "I wasn't kidding last week. I want those packets today. ASAP."

Later, in my cubicle, Joy was paging me. Her voice was everywhere in the halls, echoing, chasing. "Jay Goodpasture, it's him, line four . . . Jay Goodpasture, it's him, line three . . . It's him, line two, Jay Goodpasture, it's him . . . "

I pinched the flesh at the bridge of my nose as if I could turn on my brain by doing that. It didn't work. "The A.S.C.C. announces" became "The A.S.C.C. would like to proclaim," which evolved into "The A.S.C.C. would like to scream . . . "

"Joy, take a message, please."

"Jay Goodpasture, it's him again, line six."

"Will you please for God's sake take a message?"

"He says it's important that he talk to you now."

"Can you put him on hold?"

"Larry wants to see you five minutes ago."

"All right!" I shouted. And hit line six.

"Okay," Reginald said. "I'll turn it in at the Metro after work, but you said something about a reward."

I brimmed a hand over my eyes. "Twenty-five bucks."

The line went quiet. "Okay," he said.

Done deal! I swung back in my chair, slapped my hands together, let out a whoop, and jumped to my feet. Reginald would turn it over to the police, and an officer would bring it to our house that night. All the fear of crime, of any contact with someone who might harm us, dissipated. I felt like taking myself to lunch, but instead sat down and banged out the release. Larry loved it. Packets done.

"Well, it wasn't easy," I told Moriah that night in the kitchen of our Maple Street house. We were celebrating—a plate of Triscuits and cheddar cheese and bottles of Corona with wedges of lime. "But the thing is, you just have to negotiate hard."

The door bells chimed. She walked out to the door.

"By the way, when is Stuart's tenth reunion? Next year?"

Munching, I leaned out of the kitchen. Moriah was listening to a newspaper kid who stood under the porch light with a canvas bag of papers over his shoulder.

"We get the *Times* at the Metro stop," I called out. Glancing at my new wingtips, which I had put on for the occasion—though I was saving them for the big press conference—I strolled to the door to see if I could help her again.

The kid was wearing a Daniel Boone hat of gray imitation fur with genuine raccoon tail. Bright red Reeboks. But the hat caught my attention, because I had owned one just like it once, and I flashed back to asking my mother to buy it for me. Their tone changed into an argument, and I tuned in.

"No, see, you don't understand," he was telling her in a deep voice. "I don't want no big three-hundred-dollar box like last time. All I want is this nice little one that's only $39.95 at Radio Shack. So, what do you say?"

"I'm sorry, Reginald," Moriah said. "I will reward you because I am very thankful. I really appreciate everything you did to return my purse. But I think a twenty-five-dollar reward is plenty, don't you?"

I was aware in a distant way that I had stopped chewing, then swallowed. The fact stood before me that this was Reginald, the negotiator with whom I had struggled over the phone, but all I could do was look at the hat, remembering the way I had begged for one. And in Moriah's stern refusal to give him more money, I heard an echo of our mother's reproving penury.

"Well . . . " Reginald looked at his new Reeboks. "Twen-fi' bucks —it ain't nothing."

Moriah tore out the check, which he accepted, and I remained outside under the porch light, transfixed with some confusion. The man who had inspired such terror was a disappointed kid who strutted slowly up the sidewalk with a sack of newspapers slung over his shoulder; but for the pronunciation, I could still hear myself saying the same thing whenever I gave in to my mother. The moment of seeing what we shared was real, however transitory.

The press conference was a big success, which was a relief after the moody week had passed. Why it was such a lousy week mystified me. In softball, we finally beat the poseurs from the Soft Drink Foundation, but I didn't feel like going out for pizza with everyone afterwards. Throughout the press conference, I created a commanding presence in my Brooks Brothers suit, yellow power tie, and new wingtips. Schmoozing the reporters as they stuffed themselves with devil's food cakes, I handled them all so suavely you might have thought I was running for office. And yet, I began to feel just a bit sleazy.

"Welcome, welcome," Larry began at the podium, as though he were Reagan himself. "Welcome on this historic occasion."

"This September at Snax-Po, the producers of America's favorite action foods will call on Congress to investigate the conspiracy between foreign manufacturers to control the price of sugar. It is an issue that affects all of us, from those who are well off—" Larry waved left, to the male model behind him in the charcoal suit and yellow tie—"to America's inner-city youth"—and waved right, to the young black actor we'd hired through William Morris, who wore a ball cap sideways. "We here at the A.S.C.C. have a list of suggested import regulations we will submit to Congress at that time." He waved the list then put it down.

"In this year of hardship, then, let us all remember that good eating and good health are aspects of the good life. Like nougat and caramel," Larry said, "they're a dynamic combination. Are there any questions?"

A hand went up in the back of the group. "Are you able to name names at this point in time in terms of who you're talking about?"

"No, we are not," Larry said. "All names will be made public in September, at Snax-Po."

"Then can you tell us who you're investigating?" the same reporter asked.

"Toblerone," Larry said, "but you didn't get that from me."

The reporters wrote furiously in their notebooks. Now the questions came fast.

"Do you know how this will affect the U.S. balance of trade with the Swiss?"

"What figures have you got on tooth decay and gingivitis with regard to Europeans in terms of chocolate consumption?"

"Can you recommend a good toothpaste?"

"Are you willing to sponsor community-based, needs-oriented snack food workshops?"

It seemed that only a week earlier I had loved nothing quite so much as beguiling reporters into covering our issues and concerns, but now I had to find refuge in my cubicle. I raised the blinds. The jointed carcass across the street, that unconstructed building, was livid with crawling men in red helmets.

"Great coverage!" Larry gave me a slap on the shoulder.

"New shoes," I said. He wore a pair of wingtips, about forty dollars less expensive than mine and short in the toe.

"Here, everyone, take what you want. Little present," he said, amid the office cheer, and handed me a plastic bag heavy with fruit pies, Devil Dogs, and chocolate bars. They were all going to an early lunch; I said I would join them, took the bag with me, and elevatored down.

The clouds were breaking when I stopped outside in the June heat. For some reason I felt bereft, even sad. It was the same despondency that had plagued me all week, but now the sensation spiked, like a stereo cranked up to ten. It focused in my stomach, and patting myself there, I looked at my wingtips. And stopped breathing. In the noon brilliance they were not cordovan at all but black—dull black with bright cherry circles on the toes. I closed my eyes. I'd been cheated by the dim lights of the store.

Voices went by then got quiet—people looking at me, no doubt. Motionless with my eyes closed, I was overwhelmed with a sudden nausea of vanity. And suddenly I was in a rage, hurling galoshes across my bedroom, white socks in the garbage, a yellow raincoat into the driveway. I had to look again. The cherry toes winked this time like Raggedy Andy. My mouth went watery, and lurching down the sidewalk, I wished to God that I was someone else.

When I came to Kramerbooks, I slowed down. There, on the sidewalk, lay an elderly black man. He was asleep. One arm was bent under his head for a pillow; the other, draped across his chest, was wrapped in cellophane which formed a cone around his hand. Young men in formidable suits and popsicle ties were striding by, and as I knelt, I knew suddenly that I would not be at the council when Snax-Po came around in September.

"Trick or treat," I said, and slipped a Snickers bar inside the frayed lapel. A nice Harris Tweed, too, or it had been, and green alligator shoes. I always wanted a pair of those.

People were staring at me as they went by. All at once, with no effort on my own, they all seemed very far away, gliding back into a landscape of time, all those mental engineers and climbers driven by self-importance and issues and concerns and connections—comical and over-dressed as they went around and around, up here and down there. I had a sensation of the earth quite far beyond these immediate streets and of people and cities prospering far beyond the ambit of all these people in the important clothes and candy colors, all of whom were checking their passing reflections in store windows. I laughed out loud in the sunlight.

"Fuck it if you can't take a joke," I said, and they veered away from me.

That day I gave the bum a Devil Dog and a Ring Ding. I liked doing that small thing: life rolled out before me. Maybe I could work for a shelter, help the homeless, join the Guardian Angels, start a rock band. And maybe not. But there were thousands of trade councils, and I had always wanted to save the environment and enjoy the very simple pleasure of doing something for people.

But there was more in the bag. I slung it across my back and hiked on to Dupont Circle. Men lay in sprawling possession of the benches around the fountain and in the shade of the trees. Dry voices asked for my spare change and calloused hands received instead Twinkies, Ho-Hos, and Yum-Yums. A few of them were surly, a few threw them back or gave them away, and one of them told the others I was an ambassador on drugs. But I didn't listen. I was dispensing snack cakes. And I went on down the hot sidewalks, across boulevards, and through revolving doors, on and on, until I felt myself merging at last with the millions already circling the trees and buildings of the gleaming city.

‖‖‖‖‖‖‖ The Unfortunated
City

THE TOWN WAS SMALL AND BALANCED DELICATELY SO THAT
every change was felt unequally among us. They weren't big changes
always—events like the divorce, which came into our childhood
rooms with an astonishing shock. The world of adults was closed to us
behind bedroom doors, and the town my siblings and I knew was one
in which you could always get around on bicycle, inside a sphere of
timelessness illuminated by the colors and voices of another musty
green summer. And yet you could learn something about the adults,
even if only by an oblique remark made by your mother on the
kitchen phone one night while she boiled dinner on the stove.

"Well," she said one evening when I was seventeen and loitering
about in the doorway, "I just think that he's showing an awful lot of

interest in that retarded boy of hers to be over there every night this week." That was delicious roast-beef gossip, but however much I pleaded with her to know all the sordid details, she would not disclose them. And this was not a surprise. Years earlier, her impending divorce from my father had been something I had to discover on my own.

The space of a year was measured by the school calendar, which seemed to rise in slow spirals with bands of color for each season; eons were marked by the loss or acquisition of a family dog. "Wiggles died?" I said, aghast not so much for the amiable retriever's silent heart attack on a kitchen carpet but for the penetration of the fact that so many years had elapsed so smoothly from those warm October afternoons of touch football, when the pup retriever splashed through the gathered piles of leaves with us. Our own games always came to an end when it was time to walk uptown for the big Princeton game, where we circled through the tailgate parties, sneaked in, and threw M&Ms across the crowd. Following the usual defeat, we were part of the crowd flowing onto Canon Green, where a towering bonfire of railroad ties sent torching red sparks adrift in the green and cerulean twilight. We were a radiant crowd, threaded through by children like ourselves from other neighborhoods, talking and gossiping and looking at each other while the adults and students no doubt did the same. I frequently stood behind the others and watched the firelight dancing a Charleston on the faces of the stone gargoyles perched over the vaulted archways—a quarterback throwing a ball, kids roaring in a convertible, a blockish figure squatting and grinning in great square glasses. Stone but unweathered, they sat above us in rain and summer, darkness and dry weather; they entertained garish crowds at orange and black, brass-band reunions and played on to the sound of solitary footsteps on the flagstones when the campus was a deserted, if spacious, summer garden. "Wiggles died?" I repeated, and walked away, appalled perhaps by my own sentimentality, as though I believed a dog by that name or any other could last forever or, at best, keep pace with us although his was the short track. The simple and complex idea of death, whatever it was like to die, was an absolute; as yet, it was beyond comprehension.

As we grew up we separated out into an elementary school caste system. Those of us who arrived in town after the British Invasion were marked as newcomers and treated as such for years by those who had been weaned by the town's maternal wolf. There were fights, cliques, fallings-out, and popularity contests, and those who drifted beneath the attention of those on the social register could see a convex reflection of the town within the bevel of the classroom. And so the son of a prominent Manhattan executive became a star of our class-room kickball game, kicking in three home runs; and for one tran-scendent afternoon he felt a life none of us would know as the point of adoration for every girl in the class. He became a drummer; he became a local rock star; and I always wondered if, sometime in those burned-out years before his car wrapped around a telephone pole on the Vine-yard, killing him in the gray hours before dawn, he had ever come to think of that afternoon as the top of his life, with his every move af-terward an attempt to recover some of that lost exhilaration.

And speaking of high, how high is the Algonquin bridge? It was high enough one evening in December for a red-haired high school ju-nior to catch the attention of commuters as he stood on the handrail and stepped off into space. The local news had tape of the fireboats res-cuing him—he lived—but what shocked us was that we knew him and, what's more, that his father was a principal designer of the bridge. And this is to say nothing of the shock that slammed every household when the chairwoman of the PTA was found hanging by the neck in her basement, a suicide discovered by her four-year-old son. ("I've mopped the floor. Don't come down," the sign on the base-ment door said; but he couldn't read.) Or—just to follow this track along another curve—was anyone really surprised when Mr. X, a lawyer who lived with his battered wife and eleven contentious chil-dren in a run-down house on the corner, was indicted for using in-vestment schemes to bilk almost six-hundred-thousand dollars from some of his more greedy and gullible neighbors?

Well, we were surprised, and by all of it. There simply was no preparation for any of this. The dome of prosperity over us had been complete. On tranquil summer evenings, we ran from house to house, or skidded and jumped our Stingray bikes, while our parents wan-dered up onto neighboring lawns. "Eve, Adam—come on in. We're just having cocktails. What can I fix you?" And there in the fragrant dusk we played while the adults celebrated their arrival upon a plateau that they could not have known would become the terminus of their marriages and their ambitions. And which of us could have guessed that the scythe of cancer was on the backswing for that man there, with the white hair and pink glasses, and would swing through other numbers of us before long? If as a teenager I once labored to tear down this pleasant facade, I have long since decided I rather like the refuge to be found behind it.

And yet some people found refuge in that small town in South Dakota, where one young woman went to live with the Baghwan, in his saffron-robed community of worshippers. So alarmed were her parents, that her father, long a prominent philosophy professor at Princeton, flew out to bring her home. Only to call his wife and tell her, "I'm staying." So, the mother sent the son. But he, too, decided to join. After that, word was that the mother had collapsed into drinking and moved away, but where was anyone's guess.

For Thanksgivings, though, everyone comes back to town. The Alchemist & Barrister fills to its doors and windows with a standing crowd of returnees, adults you've known since they were the age of the shy children now standing between their knees, rather ordinary people like yourself, fat with pregnancy or bald with respectability; and yet we sort ourselves out along the same fourth-grade social lines, from bully to class clown. The town has changed almost beyond recognition now, we say. Hardware stores have become pricey boutiques. Corporations have settled down to exploit the mailing address. No one who grew up here can afford to live here. What a shame, we say, but we were tired of the town anyway. So we shake hands, exaggerate all the things we're doing, and then in the early summer do it all over again when we sneak into the university's reunion parties— adults, but still sneaking in, having our own reunion of townies, drunk, dancing, or slouched in a wooden chair and studying the comical gargoyles grinning down into the swing and lights of yet another Charleston.

Our own dining room table at Thanksgiving usually includes quite a few guests, yet however buoyant the occasion, I never know which of these extras will be here next year or how these same conversations will sound next year with still another potential mate auditioning for acceptance across the table. We don't stay as long as we used to; in a day or two, the fighting starts, and we clear out, each of us promising ourselves never to return for another holiday. It's too much. But, of course, we do. And as we eat dessert, and pick at leftovers, our mother inexorably brings up the past.

"When your Uncle Andrew and I were very little children," she begins, "we used to go down to the St. Johns' river to visit Lucky Swan."

"Who?"

The story and the question are as perennial as the opening of presents on Christmas Eve—and the disappointment over yet another dictionary and pair of gloves. Harrassing the speaker is also customary.

"Lucky Swan, stupid. Shut up and let her finish."

"He was an old man who lived on Sheep's Island near the banks of the river," she continues, "and we never knew how he supported himself, but there he lived on Sheep's Island in a shack. So we would go to visit Lucky Swan. And we would climb into an old tin washtub, push off from land using a shovel, and guide it out to the island. And there would be Lucky Swan, sitting by his fire. He used to tell us stories about Cinderella and Prince Charming, all kinds of fairy tales, and once he gave us presents."

"Is that where you got that pink Cadillac, Mom?"

"Let her finish—"

My brother Brian is now pantomiming someone pulling a long and endless something out of his mouth, and everyone laughs. Jay tells him to knock it off, and my sister, Moriah, with her new husband, Paul, tells him to ignore it.

"Go on, Mom," I say, "I'm listening. See—she loves me the most."

Our mother now looks pained, but this, too, is a traditional role she plays in these performances during holidays. Our father had a part in all this once, but that was before he saw the light and ran off with another woman, saw the light yet again and ran off with yet another woman, to resettle in Hilton Head.

"The apple crisp is delicious," says a nervous guest, an outsider visibly anxious over the verbal roughhousing. We all raise our voices and rouse our mother to go on with the story.

"Well," she says, "he gave your Uncle Andrew a catcher's mitt, and he gave me a pair of brass nut crackers shaped like a woman's legs."

Everyone laughs hard. Brian rolls his eyes at the ceiling over the symbolism, says something to Moriah, who passes the wine. Jay and I are laughing, passing the remains of the mashed potatoes.

"What was that other joint you used to go to, that Twilight Zone city?" To Jay's girlfriend and to Paul, I explain: "The place sounds like something out of Salvador Dali or de Chirico."

Everyone says they want to hear that one.

Carol sets down her wine glass and cuts into the slice of turkey on her plate, speaking as she does. "Well, when we didn't row out in the washtub to see Lucky Swan, your Uncle Andrew and I would go exploring in the woods down by Atlantic Boulevard, which is all houses today. But it was woods then, and we would go exploring there, and one day we found a deserted city. We walked out of the woods and found ourselves standing on an empty street. No cars or people anywhere. Just silence. Trees grew up out of the cracks in the pavement. There were houses with broken windows and fallen-in roofs and furniture and trees growing in the living rooms and everywhere weeds and odd pieces of clothing like boots and hats. We played there many afternoons until twilight came over the trees and houses. It had been a small company town before the First World War, and everyone moved away when the factory closed, but we didn't know that then. It was our lost town, and we called it, or I called it—because I couldn't pronounce it correctly—the Unfortunated City."

For a moment the only sound is of silver spoons cleaning china bowls. Then Brian says, "Wow, I'd love to live in a place like that." And Jay remarks, "We already do," to which there is laughter.

And once one subject comes up, there is always another.

"Hey, Mom, what's the deal with you and Uncle Jason?"

Jay asks bluntly, to laughter and protest, especially from Moriah, who tells a confused but polite Paul to forget it. But we want to know, so we listen. At least Jay has the guts to ask.

"Nothing to tell," our mother says.

"Well, what's with this letter I found once? I found this love letter once, upstairs in the den, and I was wondering, were you guys having an affair?"

The shouting is general now, everyone but me, shouting at Jay to shut his yap, which he now opens at us, full of mashed potatoes, which reminds me that I want seconds. Moriah could kill him, and it occurs to me, as I ask for the potatoes and gravy, that she and I always wanted to grow up in a different family.

"Well, did you hear about Uncle Jason's funeral?" Jay goes on. In spite of the yelling for him not to go on, go on he does, because he can yell louder than all of us with microphones. So, we all subside; and besides, we all want to hear it.

"They sprinkled his ashes down at Green Cove Springs, out by the tree—"

"You're not telling it right," says Moriah, keeper of the family genealogy and stories. "No, let me tell Paul, 'cause he doesn't know."

Jay asks for the gravy and potatoes, and I oblige.

"In the last year of his life, our Uncle Jason lived at his mother's house out in Green Cove Springs, which is this great big old house, and he began to go fishing again as a way to get his mind off the cancer. And when he was fishing, he noticed that he attracted the attention of a young hawk, so he fed it by tossing out one of the catfish he caught, there on the dock. And as the weeks went by, he went right on fishing and feeding the hawk. And soon there was another hawk and another, and Uncle Jason went right on fishing and feeding the hawks. He loved hawks cause he loved to fly—he was a pilot in the Navy for years. And when he died a few weeks ago, his last wish was that they sprinkle his ashes around the huge old water oak out there by the dock. And as they did, three hawks came circling slowly in and landed on the branches of the tree, and when the ceremony was over, each one of them lifted off, flew up in a circle a few times, and then flew away. And everyone there felt like Uncle Jason's spirit was with them."

At the end of the table, there is a subtle honking sound, and we now see our mother blowing her nose, which makes us all break out laughing. But she is serious; her eyes well up and turn red, and she waves a hand at us, because we would never understand—the hand that still wears her engagement and wedding bands. Moriah could die over the display of tears, because Paul is seeing all this for the first time. Eager to please, he now tells us that it's probably true, that Jason was flying with the hawks. Brian looks at me, and I roll my eyes at Jay. We all laugh, and Paul laughs with us, though he doesn't know why.

Now it's my turn. "Well, I remember once—down at Beersheba, when I was a kid—I came across you and Granelle talking about Uncle Jason and some love letters and Rosaline Sherman, Mom. What was that all about?"

"Rosaline Sherman," everyone says. "What's the deal with her, Mom?"

"I don't remember," Carol says, back to herself. "Paul, are you ready for dessert yet?"

"So, Stuart," Paul says later, "Moriah tells me you have your tenth college reunion coming up. You nervous?"

"He should be," everyone yells.

The evening seems endless because it is one among the numberless along a rising spiral, and we are There, and There, and There at different points around its curve, but we are there. The family was small and balanced delicately, and we did not go through every change together.

|||||||| Going Back

THE LOBBY OF ALUMNI HOUSE WAS FILLING BEHIND HIM WITH the sound of suitcases and arrivals, as he turned the registration book upside down and slid it back across the front desk.

"That's all," the receptionist told him. "But you can check later. No Stephanies."

The class of 1940 was having its cocktail party here, and from the library came the jazzy bounce of show tunes on the piano mingling with all the cocktails and voices. The atmosphere was bright with greetings between women who were white with age.

"But you were asking about the tenth? That party started over an hour ago, sir."

He could not put this off much longer. The entire afternoon of his drive up the Hudson he had anticipated the questions they would ask or, worse, the smiles when he told them. But he had unpacked, changed, and now read every magazine in the lobby. He glanced down his sleeve at a nonexistent wrist watch. "Already? My, how it flies."

Water dripping from the awning lent timbre to the piano music as he closed the heavy front door. He buttoned his navy silk blazer. The rain had cleared, leaving a sky broken with fresh light and wind. The rusticated stones of the portico were wet, pavements gleamed, and it felt good to be outside. He smoothed his emerald tie, and as though he were heading into the footlights, he started down through the gardens and the years into the weekend that lay ahead of him. Stephanie would be down there, somewhere, and perhaps the rest of his life.

His leather soles punctuated the stone silence of the buildings as he walked beneath the Douglas firs, breathing the rose-colored chill of the June sunset. The soaking greenery and twilight flashed. He stopped. It was an overwhelming—what? He looked up. They could be seen now, a skyline of silhouettes in Jewett's bay of leaded windows: the party in full swing. He was late. He would make an entrance.

"No . . . " The undergraduate ran his finger down the columns of the green computer printout. A kid. "Could you spell that?"

How many times had he wanted to say his name was Jack Gates— whose name was known by anyone who watched TV.

"Oh, see—someone penciled you in. Guess you registered late. Here's your tee shirt and your name tag. Have a nice—"

"Keep it." Stuart flipped the tag back at him.

"So, I know women who gave up finding a husband, right? And bought houses instead, like they're going to do it all anyway, by themselves. Is that fucked or what? Where are all the women?"

His roommate from senior year paused in his diatribe on being single, and they inhaled the moment on a sip of beer. It was two hours later. The campus bar was jammed—the fifth and the tenth on the dance floor and at the tables. Until Hank's arrival, Stuart had hardly spoken to anyone, and what a change. After every show on campus he used to be mobbed. But to be recognized by no one, to be invisible. And it was funny how everyone changed. Five years ago everyone was eager to show they were fast-tracking. Oh, I've got an agent now; I'm with the *Today Show.* But tonight they told him only where they lived.

Oh, we're in Greenwich now. We have a nice place in Rutherford, fifty miles from the city. Then walked away. As if in retreat from their ambitions. No one had asked him yet. Not even Hank. And his answer to both questions had begun to build. He'd had hours on the Palisades, even years, to think about it.

"Andy!"

Two hands came down his drink arm. "Andy!" And a woman slid out from behind him, arms open for a big hug. Stuart opened his arms, the usual embrace after every show.

Her smile drifted down. Stuart's didn't. Still smiling, persuaded that he knew her, he put an index finger to his mouth.

"That is so weird," she yelled.

Stuart turned to her friend, a blonde who now came around on the other side. The two women put their faces cheek to cheek as if to see what the other one saw—two lovely women, arms about waists, suspended in the red dance music and lights.

"My God," said the brunette.

"Andy?" the blonde asked.

"Sorry," the brunette called, and arm in arm they moved into the crowds in flickering movement.

"Well, that was weird," Hank said. "So, what are you—"

"Hey—there he is!" A hard, masculine arm hooked around Stuart's neck. He was nose to nose with a man who exhaled beer and Ritz and chedder into his face. "Good to see you, man. Join us. We got a table in back." He plowed away through people.

Hank said, "So, Stuart, are you still acting?"

Every explanation seemed to vanish into his drink glass; and when he glanced up from it, he could not mistake the satisfaction in Hank's face. It was not enough to succeed; one's friends must fail also.

"Well, I hear a lot from Jack every so often . . . But the job I've got now looks pretty good. It's not in theater, but I think it's pretty—"

Hank snapped his fingers by his temple. "Jack Gates, tall guy? Mr. Ivory Soap. You're still in touch with him, hunh? Isn't he starring in that new series, *Crime and Punishment*?"

On his way up the Palisades today, Stuart told himself he wouldn't do this anymore, but it did feel wonderful. There had even been times, at that wedding last year for instance, when he would talk about Jack for hours.

"Ahhhhiiiieeeee . . . " It was an Islamic shriek coming from the people around them. Everyone made way for an individual who threw his arms out to clear a space, then fell to his knees and threw himself around Stuart's knees.

"I love this man!" The prostrate man waved his hands for everyone's attention. "I worship this man! I kiss the ground you walk on!" He rose to his feet, sober. "Andrew? What? You don't recognize me? Two years in the same town house and . . . Andy, what, are you tripping or something?"

"Hank, am I having a psychotic break?"

"Andy—come on, man!" The man put one hand over Stuart's face and pressed back the lid of his right eye ball. Stuart flinched, one hand over his eye, and Hank caught him by the shoulder.

"I told you," a woman yelled over the dance music.

Stuart looked up; his eye was watering, but he was fine. The woman who yelled was the blonde. She and the brunette and others—all members of the fifth reunion—had a large round table in the corner. A large black man with them now put a hand to his cheek and hollered, "Oh, my God—you're right! It is him! Doppelganger city!" They laughed.

"Isn't it incredible?" the brunette yelled.

"Andrew—come on, cut it out. Andy, this is too weird for me. When you're done playing this little mindfuck on everyone, we'd love to see you, man—right over there."

"So," Hank said, when that was over, "you didn't answer my question."

Stuart was watching the crowd of the fifth at the large table. He felt left out, wanted to join them. "Well, we do a little import, export. Condiments we do, but mostly pickles."

"You don't even like pickles. No, I mean, do you see him anymore? Jack Gates?"

"Well, we're both so busy now, on different coasts. But it looks like he's got a deal in the works with Julia Roberts."

"Yeah, I saw that in *People*."

So, that was it; that was all. They sipped their beer and Stuart wondered why he'd bothered to come back—some reason he'd forgotten in the crush of the moment.

"There she is," Hank said. "By the fire door. She said she was going over to Mac's. You can catch up with her over there."

And there she was—he saw the curl of her profile smile out from behind the fall of blond hair. Stephanie swung that heap of color behind her shoulder and took in the bar with an exit smile that came to a pause on Stuart. Their eyes met. She stepped out into the night.

Stephanie materialized in the wet sunshine the next morning outside Main Building, and though he asked a few questions, the only thing Stuart got from her was a balloon bouncing on its red ribbon in the brilliance. She was handing them to everyone in the tenth, and the group formed a blazing splash of color in their Chinese red tee shirts and nametags. An understory of children rose amid the forest of pale legs, children in strollers, riding fatherly necks, or asleep in a maternal papoose. It was strange to see them in their new roles—all these once and future party animals—now so at ease in marriage and mortgage. And as the parade to Walker Field House began, the band booming brassy ragtime into the verdant quadrangles, Stuart was glad that he had changed his mind and come back. No one else from the drama department had come back, so he was alone. But today he would connect . . . and without being an actor. What else were reunions for, if not to show everyone that you'd escaped your past?

"You meet Vassar graduates everywhere," the tall, patrician woman in pearls told the audience. She was the jaunty chair of the board of trustees, and she commanded the microphone at the podium with an élan that said she'd spent her whole life sailing around the world. The vast audience sat in folding chairs around the gynmasium floor and roared with laughter. It was an inside joke, a family thing, greeted with the irony known only to those who belong. "Just everywhere," she went on, and the audience echoed her. "In Bloomingdale's . . . and on the Riviera."

As her suave pitch for money went on, Stuart realized that this Andy was having one hell of a fifth reunion. And, drifting into memory, he felt all over again what it was like to come back to the fifth when you had begun to make it big. It was an elation that you could never forget.

That first winter after college, the bars around Fourth Street were full of classmates who were trying to break into theater and television, magazines and advertising. Stuart got his pictures done, signed up for classes at H. B. Studios, made the cattle calls. He and Jack had a loft in TriBeCa before it was chic—going to back-beat bars within view of the derelict West Side highway and the Hudson, before the limos arrived—and his first success flashed with all his first impressions of New York.

He had gone down to the RCA building and, to circumvent the NBC guards, had taken a service elevator to the seventeenth floor. That's how he got in. All he knew was the producer's first name—Robert—so with smooth aplomb he said to the receptionist, "Hey, is Bob around?"

"Is he expecting you?"

"I hope so."

"Well, he's in a meeting. Can he call you?"

That night, after the national news, the producer did call. The brass of his approach got Stuart an interview. He met some of the cast, watched a rehearsal and a taping. And all those nights on the crowding, autumn sidewalks, in the bars with all the guys from college, Stuart was high on the belief that he was about to be cast as an extra player on *Saturday Night Live.*

It was a good story, and at the fifth reunion everyone loved it, all the old crowd, a few of whom had begun to drop acting in favor of having a life. The story was also the way Stuart answered the question: Are you still acting? And after telling the story, he would then slide into an even better one about his old friend from high school, Jack Gates, the guy he'd been sharing the loft with.

Three weeks out of Bennington, Jack landed a role on *All My Little Sisters.* Stuart wasn't envious: Jack's success would make his even more possible. But after six months Jack's character was axed by a maniac. Suddenly, he got an amazing audition to be on *The Oilmen.* Didn't get the part. Then one night Stuart came in with milk and eggs and a paper from the corner bodega. A message was on the machine. It was Jack's agent. "The other guy bombed," she said. "They want you. I bought your ticket. Your flight leaves Kennedy at 6:00 P.M. I suggest you be on it." And three months later, there he was on *The Oilmen,* a CBS ripoff of *Bonanza*—old man Faulkner's bastard son, Buck, unwrapped after an oil-well explosion—Jack Gates with amnesia.

That story really made an impression. But while his listeners were absorbed in the fantasy, Stuart would think resentfully that this was all he did anymore: wait tables and talk about Jack. But it relieved something in him to tell them, to unload the envy onto someone else, to see them turn against themselves. Success did that; it felt like a little death. Every thing good for Jack made Stuart feel like he was slowly being killed. And once Jack got going, everything came to him without his asking, and all because one person—his agent—had believed in him. She wouldn't even return Stuart's calls. He redoubled his auditions. New pictures, classes. Nothing. And yet there were great times that first year when Jack came back to New York and wore a beard and an A's cap—a ruse as ineffectual as it was obvious, and wasn't that the point?—and they were mobbed outside Studio 54. His agent procured them women, cocaine, and theater tickets. People stopped him for autographs. He posed with the owners of restaurants. Jack complained, but Stuart handled it. By then he had made his debut on the New York stage—an in-class production, but still. Now Jack's agent said she was interested.

Stuart experienced Jack's fame one night after Jack did the *Letterman* show. The elevator man recognized Jack. With an arm around the shoulders, Jack half-lifted Stuart off the floor.

"Well, do you know who *this* is? *This* is the famous actor, Stuart Goodpasture, the best Touchstone in years, the *New York Times* said."

And when the elevator man asked for his autograph—well, it was a high you never forget, a benediction. It meant that it was all about to start for him; he was next. And he'd been close, too, that was the thing of it—so amazingly close. He couldn't forget that.

So close that it was his—the life—right down to the weekend in Malibu when he watched Stephanie going down on Jack while Jack's girl went down on him. It was all theirs—and within three years of graduation . . . applause . . . the show was over.

The classes dined around the edge of the windy golf course, generations who had known war, those who had protested it, and those who studied it, everyone now eating boxed quiche and dried fruits while the incessant brass band played "Honeysuckle Rose" on into the afternoon. There were unexpected stars in their class, those in the social chorus line who had none of the campus fame Stuart had once enjoyed. They kept count. The journalist who had won a Pulitzer prize, the composer now collaborating with Andrew Lloyd Webber, the woman written up in a front-page feature in the *Wall Street Journal*. As the dogwood shadows lengthened across the mellow greens, Stuart realized that the tenth was going to be between no one but him and Hank.

"There she is. Be right back."

In the sunshine of 4:00 P.M. Stephanie stood by one of the soft-drink barrels at the entrance to the gym. She was alone.

"Oh—hey—I didn't realize that was you."

She glanced up, blond, pretty, but he could detect nothing behind the dark, heart-shaped lenses.

"Oh, there you are. Can you find any Diet Cokes? I think they're out—"

"So, you're looking well . . . "

She pulled a can up from the slushy ice. "It's always the last one. Figures, doesn't it?"

"Did you see Marissa and Alex, with three kids now?"

"I know—kind of scary, isn't it?"

"How about you. You still want kids?"

"I'm sorry . . . " Stephanie tilted her head to convey all her sympathy. Just then her hands were impossibly overfull with three cans of soda. "Maybe we can talk tonight. I'm with some friends right now. Are you staying around? Oh, good—but you look wonderful!"

The woman crossing the hot asphalt, toward people he didn't know, had once asked him to marry her. Five years ago. And he still felt a pulse of affection for her reddened heels crushing the backs of her new white sneakers, the balls of her calves as she walked in first position, the swish of her dress in the afternoon wind.

"Can we take your picture?" It was two women in the French blue tee shirts of the fifth. Stephanie glanced back, paused to watch. Stuart laughed then gave them his head-shot smile. They both snapped his picture and jogged back to a group of people moving across the soccer field.

"Congratulations," Hank said, leaning back on his elbows, when Stuart returned. "You're famous."

Stephanie had taken in the scene. She had always encouraged him, and now she had seen into him, had seen that he was still acting because he was holding onto the memory of her. Their gaze met across twenty feet of parking lot and the affection was as clear as the quality of light. Stephanie kept going but that was all he needed to see. Stuart lay back on the warm grass.

"I found her," he told Hank. "I'm there."

Midnight was an hour ago. The band was packing up its saxophones, which had been wailing and screeching to rockabilly thunder. Everyone striking equipment. Bartenders cleaning up. The kegs were dead. Beneath the tent a few determined couples were dipping each other and falling hilariously on the parquet floor. Someone put her arm around Stuart's waist, kissed his ear. She had a short cap of black hair, a little black evening dress.

"I was so happy when I heard."

"Thanks. I hoped you would be."

Hank shrugged and moved away.

She lay the carnation of her face against his lapel. "So, do you like Washington? Do you like being married?"

"I love Stephanie very much. I always have."

Her head jerked back. "I thought it was Brooke. Don't tell me you're fooling around already!"

"Ah, yes. Brooke. What was I thinking of?"

She patted his chest. "You're a good husband, Andy. I know you are. You would never fool around."

"Never."

"Not even with an old girl friend who wants you to wrap those long legs of yours around her head."

Stuart raised his eyebrows at Hank across the room. Hank tipped his glass.

"I was at Sunset Lake today," she went on, "and I remembered all those nights. That first night. Do you remember? What I did for you there? And no one else has done since. Remember?"

A tall man stepped out from under the tent. "She still can't find the Aspergum," he announced.

"This is Andy, I was telling you about. Harris, Andy."

They shook hands.

"Andy's in Senator Bradley's office. His A.A. But wants you to run for Congress, everybody says. For what? Sixth district?"

Hank waved from the road. "Everyone's going to Mac's!"

"That's great," Harris said, to Stuart. "She's looked everywhere. Is it possible you have it in your purse?"

"*Au pair* girls," she went on. "All she wants to do is get drunk and meet guys. Sounds good to me!"

"Mac's?" Stuart called back.

Crowds were forming under the wet pines. Stuart found himself pulled into the road by the drunk woman. A dark BMW stopped and she swung into the front seat. A crowd was around him now—Hank, Stephanie, and others moving up the road. Stephanie stepped out of her heels, suddenly bedroomish in her stockings, and said to Stuart, "I would love a ride to Mac's."

In the BMW the woman rolled down her window. "Andy, come on. We'll give you a ride!"

He paused between Stephanie in her stockings and the dark little beauty waving from the car.

"I'll take you," Hank said. He and Stephanie turned back toward the far side of the student center.

People calling to people, car doors slamming, and when this exodus of rubber over wet ashpalt was over, Stuart found himself walking with people he had never seen before. They followed each other loosely through the woods and came onto the state road where Mac's neon sign shone red and blue through the mist of silence.

In the bar he couldn't find that woman. But Stephanie was at the bar. Twenty minutes later they were past the amenities.

"I even wrote a novel for my creative thesis. But I just decided I didn't have anything to say. And there are too many writers like that. At least now I can do pro bono stuff."

"So, do you miss it?" he asked.

"Come on, I can't sit around feeling sorry for myself, just because I'm not Jane Austen." Stephanie turned her glass. "I think the happiest day of my life was when I just said, 'Hey, I'm not a writer.' And you can only be a promising young actor or composer or whatever for so long, and then you're not young anymore, and no one even thinks you're very promising anymore."

Stuart laughed. "You're scaring the shit out of me."

"All you need is to meet someone."

"I did."

Stephanie looked away.

"Well, I'm sorry it was so bad for you."

She smiled sweetly. "Fuck you very much, Stuart."

He laughed and sipped his beer.

"You act like I'm attacking you."

"I don't act anymore, remember?"

"Of course not. You gave up all displays of false emotion."

"Still the writer, eh?"

She watched him drink. "You know, it didn't occur to me now, but you really are an emotional cripple. Six letters I wrote—I even flew to New York to see you, you fucking bastard."

"Two postcards, and I was auditioning in Philadelphia, and I called and told you that two weeks in advance!"

"You always have to be right, don't you? Well, just keep apologizing. It just might get you there."

That was her exit line, but she didn't move. Their eyes met and they laughed into their glasses of draft beer, having to set them on the bar.

"Oh, that was fun," she said, "I haven't given you shit in years." Her right hand moved. In the past she would have brushed aside his bangs, but now she turned the glass again.

They played the moment of touching away the tears. This was a relief. Ten years ago public fights had been their inside joke, but this one was a bit close. Somehow he had lost the gauge on her inner life, and yet he felt that she was only a few words away from him now. Her green eyes, the lush black lashes and brows, the dark gold of her hair held him suspended with a sense of all he had forgotten or let go of because he could not fail at a career and be with her at the same time. He saw her eyes looking into his, searching his face compassionately.

"You know, I wasn't kidding. I worry about you sometimes." Too serious not to be joking.

"Well, that makes one of us."

"What is it you want, anyway?" Independently curious, let's clear this up. "To be famous like Jack? I'll bet you've spoken about him five times already, haven't you?"

His gaze dropped into his glass like an olive, the image of which made him smile.

"I'm serious. Whatever it is you're so angry about . . . "

He met her gaze.

She touched his cheek with the back of her fingers. "You know, it's always self-pity or fantasy with you. You have to like yourself more and do something with your life. You can't just find a woman and a career like that. You have to exorcise your ghosts, Stuart. All that family shit haunting you. Get off stage—" Stephanie stopped herself, realizing that this wasn't a conversation any longer but the accumulated advice of five years of silence.

This time there was no joke, and they had come to the end of whatever was between them—more pity than concern.

"I'll talk to you later," she said, and moved off into the crowds of married couples in the tenth, around the pool table.

Left by himself with the locals, Stuart played it off as if nothing had happened. Stephanie stood with Hank, watching him, and so to amuse her, he went into his Bogart: lit a cigarette, inhaled and squinted, then stubbed it out dead on the bar.

"What are you—a mime or something? That was wonderful!"

It was the blonde and the brunette, like twins on a single barstool. "Henry—it's Andy. Come here. You have to see this."

From the next table a large black man came over, the man who had bellowed comically the night before. "Oh, my God! He really does— even up close! But you're an actor, right? I mean, that was wonderful. Improv, am I right?"

"H. B. Studios," Stuart said. "Six years."

"So, are you still acting?" the brunette asked.

Stuart smoothed his tie. "Well, I wanted to get off the stage. But a good friend of mine is doing pretty well. Maybe you heard of him. Jack Gates."

"Oh, my God. *The Oilmen*, right? God, he was so cute. Henry— Henry—pay attention here. He's friends with Jack Gates."

The enormous Henry, who had dipped into another conversation, now devoted himself exclusively to the one with the famous name. "Really? You know Jack Gates? My sister's real good friends with him. We were all up at his place on the Vineyard last August. Beautiful place, right on the water. Have you seen it?"

"I've heard it's gorgeous." Stuart twisted his neck.

"How does your sister know Jack?" the brunette asked.

"She's at William Morris," he went on. "Your basic talent agent.

She loves it! Talk about perks. But she says it's like, once one of these guys makes it, all their friends try to climb on board. Quelle drag! So she just feeds them a line. Yadda yadda yadda—then blows them off."

"That's awful," the blonde said.

"So, where do you know Jack from?"

Stephanie and Hank were leaning over the pinball machine, rather cozy together. "Jack? We were in high school together."

"And what's your name again? Well, I'm sure he mentioned you. My mind is just . . . " Henry flitted his fingers.

The women seemed willing to listen if he wanted to talk about Jack. Stuart felt himself come back into focus; felt the old posture come back. "We shared a loft in TriBeCa. Ran lines together. I was still—"

"Oh, oh, oh, oh!" Henry pointed his finger at Stuart's nose. "You're the one. Was it *Saturday Night Live* was going to hire you?"

The women looked at Stuart and he felt himself shift into contraposto. He was no longer just the man who resembled their friend. A landscape of success, of being, took shape around him.

"It's a great story, actually. I was—"

"Oh, this is great!" Henry framed the scene with his large open hands. "You had this thing, right? Like an interview, but like they weren't really interested? And then Jack called my sister and said it was him they wanted, right? He said it so he could meet her and it worked. So they meet for lunch and they really hit it off, and she sends him over for that part on *Little Sisters* and that's how he got his start. The rest is trivia history!"

"You think he's any good?" the blonde said.

"As an actor?" asked the brunette.

Stuart felt the strain in his smile, as his gaze dropped into his glass of beer. It would take him days to go through what he had just heard, compare the perfidy with what he knew.

"That's why I love New York, it's all so . . . " Henry crinkling his fingers.

"He's very wooden," the brunette said. "Lifeless."

"You know, lots of famous actors lived together when they were starting out in New York. Paul Newman and Marlon Brando."

"And Robin Williams and Superman."

"And Katharine Hepburn and Robert DeNiro."

"And Erich von Stroheim and Paul Anka."

They were in hysterics. Henry said, "You know, he really does look like Andy—especially now when he's, like, spacing out? Oh, oh, oh! I can't believe I didn't tell you the best part. End of August and guess who we bump into outside of Edgartown? Andy! Yes! And he's with Ted Kennedy, and guess where we see them? On the bridge to Chappaquiddick! Yes! It's true! They're selling pieces of it, and he's got Ted to autograph each one!"

The women roared. "You are so full of shit," and they tried to push him away.

"Yes," he said emphatically. "But it's really good shit!" Henry put a hand to his chest. "I swear to God, you see Vassar grads everywhere! Could you believe that speech today!"

"So, wait—" The brunette put up her stop-sign hand. "What I want to know is—Martha's Vineyard, did everyone look at Andy and say, Oh, my God, it's . . . it's—"

They all looked at Stuart, who looked up. "Uh—Stuart Goodpasture, but we dropped the 'uh' two hundred years ago."

They roared.

"See—that's why you should have been on *Saturday Night*," Henry said. "That shtick you did before was brilliant!"

Stuart pulled another out of his hat: a man bumping into a glass wall, his face going mush. They brayed and roared. Hank and Stephanie watched in silence. Stuart backed up and tried another. He got his tie caught in a revolving door; got dragged in circles; went backwards, forwards, face mashed against the glass. The blonde put her hand over her mouth, and they almost got her to spew beer through her nostrils, she was laughing so hard.

The brunette breathed into his face. "You look the way Andy would want to look on the very best day of his life!"

"Remember that time Andy and Zen tried to fly off the roof of the townhouse? They'd been 'shrooming for a week, and they were so fucked it was amazing!"

They all began to flap their arms. Everyone in the fifth was laughing, some fifty people at the tables around them. "Andy was so fucked. Here, you do it—come on—like this!"

Stuart refused. Henry demanded. Other voices yelled, and suddenly, Stuart sent his hands out to his sides and did a quick swoop.

"No, no, no, no!" Henry megaphoned. "More emotion! Hey—check it out!" He yelled. "Andy's flying!"

The entire audience of the fifth watched, amid the jukebox rock-'n'-roll, the smoke of cigarettes, the click and smack of pool balls. Stuart gave a wide aircraft swing of his arms. The roar of laughter, swinging around, each time glimpsing Stephanie and Hank. "Keep going!" Henry yelled.

That was enough. Stuart bowed, one hand across his stomach. The one he graciously folded behind his back for the bow upended the waitress's tray. Three pint glasses of beer hit the floor.

For a second the waitress, hassled all night, stared at him. Then she smacked the tray on the bar. The glasses hadn't broken. Stuart picked them up. More applause, cheers. Henry disappeared into someone else's conversation. The space of wooden panelling beside the pinball machine was blank now; Hank and Stephanie were gone.

"Whoops-a-daisy," said the blonde. "So, what about you? If you're not Andy and you're not Jack Gates, who are you? I see you don't have a name tag."

"What do you do?" said the brunette. "Anything interesting?"

"Uh, Import, export. But we—"

"Dropped the 'uh' two hundred years ago?"

"—do condiments mostly. Red Apple. Food Town."

"What, toilet paper?" The women couldn't believe how awful they were being and thumped each other on the thigh, laughing.

"Mostly pickles."

"So, what do you do when you meet women?" said the blonde. "You just talk about Jack all the time, or what?"

"He shows them his pickle." The brunette yanked Stuart's silk tie. "Green suits you. Look." She drew back his jacket to reveal the beeper on his belt. "That's so his wife can find him," she said, and they collapsed, head to head, with laughter. And when they didn't notice that he was moving away, Stuart set his glass down and kept going.

Somewhat drunk and very weary, he wavered along the side of the state road through the chill June mist—alone as he hadn't been since college. But what were reunions for if not to revisit the past? At Jewett he slowed down. Beside a large tree stood a man and woman embracing. The kiss was tentative but felt. They turned toward Sunset Lake, the traditional spawning ground, and as they walked beneath the red light of the fire exit, Stuart saw that they were Hank and Stephanie.

In the morning they were all there, all the new old crowd, those acquaintances who had fashioned themselves into cliques for the sake of a weekend. In the damp sunshine outside Jewett, they sat on the grass in circles of reserved conversation, making a breakfast of bagels and fruit salad, and sousing hangovers with citrus juice and caffeine. A few men were tossing a frisbee; a black lab, with a red bandana around its neck, was chasing it—the son of the dog who had been on campus a decade ago—and it was a picture of college life. But those once frizzy were now bald, and those once sleek were now round. Women sat with babies between their knees, changing diapers, talking children. And everyone seemed relieved that it was over. They had been out longer than they had been in, and were ready to return to their lives.

Stuart sat with them. He was cured. Exuberant as he hadn't been in years, he learned that he wasn't the only one who didn't know what to do with his life, who was still looking for a woman to love and a career to pursue. He recovered his nametag from the registration desk, where it sat alone. Seated with Hank and Stephanie, but talking to everyone else in the group, he had the sustained detachment now of many years, of looking back on all this, and the first night came back to mind. It was the lapse of years that had shocked him, in juxtaposition to the sameness of the campus. That was the quality he had sensed that first night while walking to the cocktail party. Places had been ephemeral while his youth had felt like forever. But now he was beginning to zoom through a landscape that had begun to stand still.

A woman went by, lugging a caterwauling child by the hand.

"I'd rather have cats."

"Oh, I love cats! I have three myself. Here," and dipping into her purse, Stephanie came up with photos of a kitten sitting in a cereal bowl. Everyone, and they were all single, shared stories about their dogs and cats.

"So, Hank, what are you up to these days?"

"Living on an island in Maine," he said, "with my dog."

"Why am I not surprised?" Stephanie said, to congenial laughter. And Stuart could see that whatever friendship they had cashed in on the night before had been spent.

The light of five o'clock was glancing down through the beeches around the Alumni House cafe when Stuart came out to the car. His suitcase he slung into the trunk, jackets he hung up, green tie, red tee shirt, and name tag he tossed in the backseat. He went inside and wandered into the library. The baby grand piano was gleaming black. Beneath the leaded windows, columns of light were blazing in medallions of colors on the Persian carpet—all very faded but beautiful. That mixer had been here freshman year, the one where he met Stephanie and Hank. And suddenly the stillness clicked with all the exhilaration of starting out with everyone toward everything. They became anything they wanted to be—artists, writers, and actors— stunning transformations in one semester and anyone could do it. Which is why everyone did it. His voice was quiet in the bright silence. "Was that ten years ago already? My God, where have I been?"

The sound of rap was coming from the kitchen when he dropped his key at the front desk. The woman closed the heavy doors behind him to preserve the air conditioning. He was late now. Traffic on the Palisades would be heavy. He would be caught in the slow, exhausting pace with everyone else. Before he went down to his car, Stuart set his palm on the rusticated stone of the portico, now hot with sun, and gave it a flat, clear smack in the silence while he was still there.

||||||| The Visit

WELL, OF COURSE, WE WOULD FRIGHTEN BUBSY, BUT I wanted Jay to crack my back. So while we waited for her to answer the chimes, we went back to back, my brother and I, and linked our elbows. Jay rolled me up on his back and began jerking me up and down, and we stumbled and laughed an awkward dance across the bright front porch. The December morning was mild with a visible moon, my spinal disks were snapping, and before us lay a quick and dirty visit with old Bubsy, after which we had to be back across town for lunch with our cousin Tom. We felt so good, Jay and I, that we couldn't resist horsing around. And, besides, alarming Bubsy is a respectable family sport: my father, Aunt Betty, and first cousins all do it. Jay and I were laughing because Bubsy would no doubt flutter into a panic when she opened the door to find an apparition: two strange men struggling like Laocoon on her welcome mat.

"Take it easy," I said, as the heavy door drew in over the carpet.

"Oh, my goodness, now what's all this? Oh, dear . . . "

Jay dropped me and threw open his arms for the kind of reunion we never have with our father's side.

"Bubsy!" he called out. "Remember me? I'm your grandson Jay!"

"Be careful," she told me. "Stay out of my flowers."

I caught my balance against the column.

Bubsy said, "Who did you say you were? Jay!" And she lit up, tickled pink to know who he was. She placed a hand to her throat, saying, "Of course I remember you." But then she looked at me and started shaking her anxious bracelets, and I saw fear in her blue eyes.

"And Stuart," I told her. I shook her hand in the solicitous manner of an old family lawyer come to break bad news. "So good to see you again, Bubsy, dear," I went on. "We've come for a little visit."

Jay and I started in, but Bubsy stopped and we all piled up in the doorway.

"Well, you called first, didn't you?" she said. "Because you know, sometimes I have to go to the hairdresser's."

"Of course, Bubsy, dear," I said. And with a hand on her frail shoulder, I guided her back inside. "Would we impose?"

As she and Jay paused to examine family pictures on the wall, it seemed to me that somehow Bubsy had stopped getting older. She appeared on this mild winter morning to be the same nervous little woman who had answered the chimes on summer mornings when I was seven, then seventeen, and on all the days between when we came for a visit. In the last decade, others of her generation had died off— her husband and brother-in-law, to name only two—but here she was, unaltered by either time or circumstance as far as I could discern: little Bubsy of the piano legs smiling nervously under her chandelier, her blue curls, her hands shaking the same anxious bracelets. In her gray eyes and long face I saw the features of a dead movie star, but I couldn't quite identify the famous face hidden in her own.

Nor could I believe that ten years had passed since I had last seen Bubsy. That was the year my parents divorced, and after a nuclear exchange of words, their families stopped speaking. A tremendous number of unbelievable stories branch from my father's family tree—that woebegone family of Goodpastures with their lunatic visions. But to be succinct, what happened five years ago was that my father drove down from Princeton to Jacksonville to handle Bubsy's business with the First Federal Bank of Florida—which was then stealing orange groves from her—and during his visit, his sister (our Aunt Betty) introduced him to a pretty blonde friend of hers. She was a perky, tennis-playing, born-again Christian. And in no time father ran off with her to preach the gospel in Mexican prisons. And not since that winter had any of us children had any traffic with my father's side of the family, and especially not with our Aunt Betty.

Which this year, and on this occasion, now seemed a little silly and sad. My mother's brother had died, and our rather large Southern family was converging on Jacksonville. The gathering was huge, and yet everyone pretended we weren't here for a funeral, which made my dead uncle's absence all the more felt and telling. One night in the living room, with everyone else speaking very sociably, I seemed almost on the verge of seeing his face, of hearing his voice, or meeting his thoughts in some way. I even put my plate in my lap and looked toward the dining room, but my Uncle Andrew—whom I loved as though he were my father—did not materialize in the dining room doorway, though somehow he did seem to be standing there, in that old tennis sweater and those paint-covered khakis.

Southern politeness can sometimes seem so phony that you want to start a scene; and when my brothers, Brian and Jay, and I realized that old Bubsy was getting up there, we decided to cross the Ortega Bridge into the deep shadows of Jacksonville for a quick visit. So there we were on a benign morning, with no idea of who was waiting for us in the living room, but we wanted to make peace with Bubsy before she, too, was gone.

"She won't even know who you are," our mother said querulously in the kitchen that morning.

Perhaps not, but we would know who Bubsy was, and that was the point.

"Well, come in, come in," Bubsy went on, as we came inside. She threw two dead bolts, turned the key, and hung the chain.

She and Jay went on into the twilight whispering with air conditioning and roaring garishly with some game show on the television, but I remained by the door and began superimposing the past upon the present in an extemporaneous search for ghosts.

This was the same Persian-carpet hallway to the bedrooms where we had run as children and the same studio photographs of Bubsy and Grand Billy, and Great Uncle Howard, painted with dead fleshtones. Wedding pictures—Aunt Betty, back when she was a dark beauty of nineteen, in bridal gown on the grand staircase of the Yacht Club, with her train in a circle around her feet. And there in the next photograph were my own parents, on the same grand staircase, my dark father and blonde mother, in tuxedo and gown and radiant with the cinematic beauty of youth. All three of them were absolutely gorgeous almost thirty years ago when they could never have known that they were starting off toward bitter divorces and hateful children who would one day say rotten things about them to almost anyone.

"Oh, Stuart," Jay sang out. "Why don't you come in and join us?"

And then the grandchildren's photographs—of my cousin Heather, looking like a hippie while strumming a folk guitar. I had such a crush on her years ago; I would love to see her again, but we didn't have time today. Still, I rather hoped she would appear somehow. School pictures of Jay and of our older sister, Moriah. And then two Cub Scouts: Brian and I, touching our caps in a salute to our grandmother, Bubsy, who took us to the Yacht Club for Labor Day dances and club sandwiches . . .

"Keep your shirt on," I said, and went into the living room.

"Well, surprise! There he is! I was just telling Jay that it has been so long since I've seen you! Oh, and you've grown so much. When Bubsy said you all had called, I just had to come right over and surprise you! Bet you didn't expect to see me! Give me a big hug!"

Aunt Betty. Dark and huge. Leaning on the dining room table with her fist. Then I saw her ghost on the dining room wall behind her—that lurid, romantic portrait of her at nineteen. In the foreground, leaning on the table, the actual Aunt Betty had grown tangled and heavy, engrossed with snarls of black hair.

Jay was bugging his eyes at me, the exact sense of which I lost, because Aunt Betty had begun to move. She was now gliding across the carpet, her scales of green silk glittering in the track lights. Before I could think, she coiled her arms around me and began to suffocate me against her deep, Victorian bosom. My back began to pop again. One disk, then another. Jay raised his eyebrows, to which I answered by raising my own.

"Well, come in, come in, sit down," Aunt Betty said, and we all sat down a bit stiffly. "I'm so glad to see you, but I'm so sorry it had to be on this sad occasion."

"Sad occasion?" Bubsy's eyes dilated with fear.

"Mo-ther!" Aunt Betty slung her jaw slack like someone who knows how to deliver a wise crack, or grew up watching movie stars deliver them in Saturday matinees. "Mo-ther, I told you." And rolled her eyes.

"Told me? Told me what?" Bubsy laughed but worried her bracelets. "Goodness gracious. You hear so many things you just can't keep up with them all. Oh, me . . . " And smoothed her floral dress over her one-time flapper's knee.

No one talked. We all turned to the console television. On the game show, a man dressed as a tomato was telling the world he was from Short Pump, Virginia.

"So," Aunt Betty said. "Where are Brian and Moriah? They're not snubbing us, are they?" We all laughed—ha, ha, ha. Jay and I agreed in one glance: Aunt Betty had fired the first shot.

Jay explained that Brian was just up the street, visiting his godfather; Moriah was flying down tomorrow; and while they went on, I tried to square the material Bubsy seated on the floral sofa with the legendary one of so many dreadful stories. It was hard to believe that this woman in the mortuary makeup had once been a popular debutante. I tried to run back her life-movie to the day when she threatened my father and Aunt Betty that, if they didn't stop fighting at the dining-room table, she would run away, then locked herself in the bathroom, climbed out the window, and spent a week with her sister only to return to two terrified and grieving children. "If you don't stop that fighting," my father once told Brian and me, as we kicked in the bathtub, "I'm going to leave and never come back." He then brought a suitcase into the hallway, and we went into hysterics that took my mother all night and several days to mollify. And I don't believe Moriah ever forgave him. I looked at the pats of rouge on Bubsy's cheeks, the shadow of mustache and sideburns, and I blamed her for my father. And with incremental bitterness, I realized who she reminded me of—Bing Crosby in drag.

"What's so funny?" Jay said.

"Nothing."

Bubsy, Bubsy, Bubsy—what a name. When my father was ten years old, she packed him off to Atlanta to be raised by Great Uncle Howard because she was too distraught to raise a boy. Even when I was ten years old, she insisted that she dab my pecker after I whizzed. But she never changed my diapers when I was a baby.

"Don't be silly," my other grandmother said that morning in the kitchen. "The neighbors had to come over and do it. Yours, Brian's— and your father's and Betty's."

"I'd leave you two with her for the afternoon," my mother said, pouring coffee, "and I'd come back and you'd both be crying and neither Bubsy nor Betty, neither one, had changed your diapers all day. They'd just let you sit there crying until I got there."

And it gets worse. The common belief on my mother's side is that Bubsy drove Grand Billy into both his strokes, which left him limping on a cane and sleeping away his afternoons at the age of forty-three. "You don't want to be a failure like him, do you?" Bubsy said to my twenty-year-old father, and jerked her thumb over her shoulder at her husband napping on the same sofa where, some thirty years later, she was watching a game show on a mild December morning.

"And Grand Billy was such a sweet, gentle man," my mother said at the breakfast table. "He and your Great Uncle Howard were always kind and generous to you all."

My grandmother said, "I remember Howard telling me once about visions he had. Yes—he told your grandfather and me one night that ancestors came to see him. You know, I think he honestly believed he was haunted by ghosts. Oh, we had such a laugh over that, your grandfather and I. And I think all those Goodpastures have a touch of that. They're all a little . . . you know . . . " She arched her eyebrows and shrugged. "Unstable."

Still, they were kind fanatics. Grand Billy used to take Brian and me for endless walks along the Ponte Vedra beach to look for sharks' teeth on bright August afternoons. We couldn't understand his speech very well, but he showed us rare shells and smiled. Then back at the beach house—which Aunt Betty has since taken illegally from us— he added our new shells to his careful patterns arranged on black felt inside the glass tables—the same glass tables upon which this morning Aunt Betty was just now clacking down cups of coffee and plates of iced banana bread.

"So, how is everyone?" Jay asked Aunt Betty.

Undeniably, I think, the worst story is what Bubsy did to our Great Uncle Howard, her brother-in-law. For almost forty years he was a genial librarian in Ponte Vedra, one of those harmless old guys who seem to take a seat early on outside the dance floor of life. He lived with his two sisters—Jule and Amy, Grand Billy's other siblings—and it was a curious arrangement from the nineteenth century. Not one of them ever married, and they grew old together. As a child I met them in the windy brilliance of a summer afternoon, but I was unable to place them in the family; my only impression was of the sisters' wireless glasses, lace doily collars, deep, low bosoms, and pearl necklaces, and of Great Uncle Howard's crisp white yachting cap and the kindness of his aqueous blue eyes.

Great Uncle Howard and his sisters lived quietly and modestly on the orange grove trust, and then as Hitler annexed Austria and it was clear that the Antichrist had come, that surely some revelation was at hand, that surely the Second Coming was at hand, they gave away their share of the orange groves to some maniacal zealot in California —the great I AM. Then, on a warm, wind-washed evening in April, they walked down to the banks of the St. John's river. There, among the incidental shadows of pines and transient wind, they sat on a wooden dock and waited. The blue air was cool. The sun was setting. The last sunset over the earth was magnificent: an incandescent firestorm rising in red towers into the clouds. And they waited on through hours of darkness and starlight for the world to come to an end.

Well, of course, they were premature in their calculations, or, rather, their zealot was, but the groves of family wealth were gone and unrecoverable.

"They were poor, sweet, simple people," my father said of them, a bit melodramatically and not very long before he, too, followed form, had his vision, and ran off to preach in the jail cells of Tijuana. I cannot say precisely what his vision was, but in the strangely quiet week before he left us, my father one night looked up from his armchair where he sat reading a book. He looked at the dining-room doorway. "Howard?" he said. He blinked twice, his eyes widened with some emotion, and he got up to fix himself a drink.

Anyway, with the money gone and with his sisters in their graves, Great Uncle Howard found himself living in the poverty of Social Security benefits. One summer afternoon Bubsy answered her chimes to find him standing there. Surprise! He'd come for a little visit! Could he come in? They sat in the living room. Could he come live with them? He couldn't pay rent, but he was clean and . . . and he didn't get any further.

"You think I don't have enough on my hands with one old man to look out for?" Bubsy said. "Of course you can't live here."

She threw Howard out, and more: she didn't tell Billy that his brother had come looking for a place to live. Howard dropped from sight and a year later, after my father fixed his drink that night, we received a phone call from the old family lawyer who informed us that Howard had died that evening of a stroke.

"Well, son," my father told me, long distance from Jacksonville after the funeral, "it seems your Great Uncle Howard tried to walk into the sea someplace near Ponte Vedra, but some of these hippie types that smoke marijuana saw him and stopped him. Seems they took him to live with them in one of those communes of house trailers and teepees out there in the pine woods. And I only found out when I met a few of them at his funeral, son. What? No, Bubsy never told me. Yes, she knew. 'Cause she told me she disapproved of them. I just don't know what makes mother act that way."

He was silent.

"Well, son, I gotta run," he said, without apparent irony. "Take good care of your mother," and that was the last anyone saw of him.

In that adolescent winter of death and elopement, Brian and I began to despise dear old Bubsy, to blame her for everything. And on this December morning I remembered my last scene with her one December morning ten years past, shortly after my father had run off with Muriel, the born-again Christian.

"Oh, dear," Bubsy said the day of that last visit. "I just don't know what makes your father act the way he does."

Grinding my braces, I said, "Maybe, Bubsy dear, it has something to do with the way some woman raised him."

Brian started shaking his head, "No, no, no," and Jay, who was too young then to feel real hatred, said, "Shut up, Stuart; you don't know what you're talking about."

"Of course not," I said.

But I continued to glare into Bubsy's powdered face that day ten years ago, and on this morning I found myself glaring at her still. And, my God, what a crime it seemed that my Uncle Andrew should die of cancer at fifty-two while Bubsy dithered peacefully on into her eighties, never punished or told off, irrelevant except when a she was a nuisance.

"Well," Aunt Betty was saying just then, "did you all get the silver? We mailed you each a silver spoon."

As I now came spiraling up into the moment, through all those convoluted memories, I wondered where we were and what we were talking about. Silver? What silver? I opened my eyes. Jay was raising his eyebrows at me, to which I responded with a dull frown. An old family theme, their robbery of the family silver.

"Sure did," I said. Then realized that we hadn't.

"And thanks for the checks, Bubsy," Jay said.

"Checks?" She looked frightened.

"Well, Christmas isn't over yet," Aunt Betty said. "We got you some more presents, didn't we?" She nodded at the coffee table, where sat three boxes in glossy red paper and green bows that had appeared out of nowhere.

"Now, this one's for Brian," Bubsy said. "Are you Brian?"

"Mother! That's Jay. Brian isn't here yet—though I don't know what could be keeping him." She giggled.

"Are you Brian? Well, where's Brian? I have his present for him. Are you Brian?"

"Mother, relax. He isn't here yet."

"Wasn't that him? I thought he was in the dining room."

"Mo-ther, you're imagining things." Aunt Betty did her eye roll. "We got you all the same thing. Furchgott's was having a sale." And smiled cute as Shirley Temple.

Bubsy smiled as though the world was just moving too fast. "You know, you all have gotten so big and grown up, and there's so many of you, I just can't keep up with you all. Oh, me . . . " She laughed and smoothed her skirt over her knee.

"Oh, wow, this is great," and I recognized in Jay's voice the sound of our father's phony enthusiasm. "It's a dop kit with nail clippers, a comb, and everything. Open yours up, Stuart." He was almost yelling.

"Mother, why don't I turn that down?"

On the television, Tomato Man was trying to guess the price of green beans, a task just then beyond his vegetable powers.

Bubsy went stumping across the room. "Well, I don't know how you can turn it down. Maybe I should turn it off. Are you watching it?"

"Two dollars," Jay said.

"A buck seventy-five," I said.

Bubsy played with the knobs. The picture went green.

"Mother, please, I have the remote control!"

Bubsy turned a knob and applause hit us like the backwash of a Concord jet at takeoff. We grabbed our ears, yelling. Bubsy turned another knob. The picture began to bleed red.

And yet, curiously enough, this was a relief to the conversation. "Bubsy," I yelled, "let's leave it on!"

"Are you watching it?" she hollered.

"No!"

"Mother! Mother!" Aunt Betty yelled through the megaphone of her hands, and suddenly I saw her at the beach house, calling us in from the water. She aimed the remote control and blasted us into—

Silence. Emptiness before creation. Silence of the void after time has ended. Dust could be heard falling loud as rain through the soft air. Then the ringing started, sirens in both ears. Pulled at my ear lobes; shook my head sideways. Jay was doing the same. We looked at each other, wondering.

"Oh, there we go," Bubsy said. "I've got the sound turned down. But now the color's all wrong . . . "

Jay bounded across the room, slipped into her arms, and danced her back to the sofa. Aunt Betty aimed again. The TV winked with astonishment and died.

"So hard to tell what's going on, what with all that racket. I don't know how you all can watch the television that way. I know I never could." Bubsy laughed and smoothed her skirt. "Oh, me . . . I guess I'm getting old. Everyone wants to be a hippie. But I don't like all that long hair on boys, do you? They look like girls to me."

Bells chiming. "I'll get it!" And bolted out.

Door opening—Brian had materialized. He stood there with his fists thrust into the small of his back, cracking it.

"Where the hell have you been?" I said. "We have to get out of here and like right now—"

"What do you guys think of that?" Jay yelled.

"Oh, there he is. Why, Brian, what a beard. I never would have recognized you. Come give me a great big hug—"

"Aunt Betty," Brian said, with our father's fake enthusiasm.

Aunt Betty encoiled him powerfully and burped him with several meaty slaps on the back.

"Think of what?" I said.

"Having lunch with Heather," Jay said, coming into the foyer. "You had a crush on her, didn't you, Stuart? That's what you told me, that you really had the hots for her back when you were a feeble little dork in the eighth grade."

I gave Jay the cold gaze, as though with a glance I could turn the volume down.

Aunt Betty explained how she had made plans for us that would get us into scalding water with our mother's side of the family.

"It's been so long and we never get to see you, and I know Heather wants to see you all so badly. Mother get your coat on, dear; we're going to lunch. So, what do you say? My treat. We'll go to the Yacht Club like old times. Remember when you were children? The fun you had there? The Labor Day dances? You still like club sandwiches? Wonderful, then it's all set. I'll just call Heather and tell her we're on the way."

"Call Tom," I told Brian. "Tell him we can't make it for lunch today."

"You call him," he said to Jay.

Jay said to me, "You call him."

I said to Brian, "You call him."

In the living room, Bubsy and Aunt Betty were gliding around the furniture, telling each other what to do.

"They dragged us into it," I muttered.

"Shut up, Stuart," Jay said. "You don't know what you're talking about."

"Bubsy, hi," Brian said. He threw open his arms for the kind of reunion we never have with our father's side. "Remember me? I'm your grandson Brian."

Bundled in a winter coat, Bubsy walked out between us.

"Stay out of my flowers," she said.

1 1

And then we were doing almost seventy miles an hour down Atlantic Boulevard in the bright windy traffic, Brian trying to find the magical speed that would unlock all the green lights. So we were booming through yellow ones. Bubsy was yelling that we should slow down. Aunt Betty pooh-poohing her. Then bam: there it was, a red light, stationary traffic. Brian began pumping the brakes of Bubsy's Buick dinosaur—pump, pump. They grabbed and slam—we all fell forward.

"What the hell are you trying to do?" Jay yelled.

"What's that noise?" Bubsy cried. "I hear a noise!"

"Oh, Mother, hush. You're imagining things. Next thing you know, she'll be seeing ghosts." Then giggled.

As we went bombing along, the malls washed out in the winter brilliance, I looked at Aunt Betty, who was looking out the open window. Still pretty, and when she drew hair behind her ear, I suddenly saw nineteen-year-old Heather in a car full of wind, tucking hair behind her ear. Heather was about five years older than I was and had both huaraches planted in the sixties. How I had worshipped her. She wrote songs on her folk guitar, wore bell bottoms, and smoked grass. She found an alley cat and named it Freedom. The adults couldn't bear to have her around, and she soon dropped out of high school. She was flip, uncooperative, peevish, and vulgar. And I loved her madly.

"Hey, how is Heather anyway?" I yelled. "I haven't seen her in, God, maybe ten or twelve years."

Aunt Betty tucked hair behind her ear. "Well, you know she married that professional bowler? God. I don't want to sound critical, but that Gary's a disaster. He's never had a job. All he's ever wanted to do is bowl. He's Mr. Big Dreams. Next week something'll happen, next month. You're clear," she yelled to Brian, and we went sweeping across three lanes to avoid a slow semi. Bubsy's rattles were shaking. "Anyway, it's gotten so that we don't even ask what he's up to. It's sad, very sad. He doesn't even have a job, and it's been this way for ten years. My God, he's going to be thirty-eight. Poor Heather. I told her not to

marry him, but she had to spite me. I just thank God she's not preg-
nant—"

We bumped across railroad tracks into a glaring district of flat-
topped warehouses and hurricane fences. The international headquar-
ters of Winn-Dixie Supermarkets looked like an old 1950s public
high school building.

"There she is, by the door," Aunt Betty said. "And she's in a mood;
we must be late. Now act like I didn't say a word. She gets so put out
with me sometimes."

Gone was the frizzy hair, Indian print skirts, and huaraches, but
there was the old attitude. Heather came stomping into the windy
brilliance on stiletto heels, her frosted hair flying back over her padded
shoulders. Her red, slit skirt was flashing some lovely thigh. She
flicked her cigarette into the street and opened Jay's door up front.

"Where am I supposed to sit?"

"Up front, silly." Aunt Betty did her eye roll.

"There isn't any room up here. Brian, shove over."

"I'm Jay."

"How am I supposed to know? You all look so much alike. Now
shove over; I only have an hour." She swung her black purse in, followed it, and slammed the door. "Stuart, God, when did you grow a
beard? You look like Jerry Garcia."

"I'm Brian."

"I thought I saw you in my office doorway," Heather said. "Anyway,
one hour. I can't believe it. That jerk, Bobby? The new guy? He
thinks he can tell me when to take lunch. Well, screw him. I'll quit
first. I'll disappear. Besides, I told him today was special—my cousins
were in town. God, you guys have gotten so huge. Moriah didn't
come, did she? I knew it."

"Aren't they huge?"

"So, Heather," Jay said. "What do you do for Winn-Dixie? Sell orange juice?"

Heather snorted, lit a fresh cigarette. "Always were a little smartass,
weren't you? Or was that Stuart? Is he here?" She turned around; I
smiled at her. "Oh, there you are. I thought I saw you in my office doorway. Mundo bizarro. Brian, this is a red light; you might want to stop."

Pump, pump, pump—grab—skid—and we all fell forward.

"What's that smell? I smell something burning!"

"Oh, Mother, hush. You're imagining things."

"Actually," Brian said, "I believe I see smoke coming from that corner of the hood."

"We're okay," Heather said. She turned and faced us over the seat. "This bomb'll run forever. Hell, Bubsy only drives it to the hairdresser's once a week. Speaking of which, when's the last time you went, Bubsy? We're looking a little greasy today." She rubbed a Bubsy curl between her fingers, snorted with disgust, and wiped her fingers on the vinyl.

"I smell smoke. I smell something burning."

"Oh, Mother, hush."

And then we were doing almost eighty-five, but still the magic wouldn't happen and red lights chased us as we shot through yellow ones, chasing green ones. Stop light, but this time plumes of smoke came from under the hood. Bubsy put her hands to her cheeks and her mouth made an "O" as she cried out.

"Oh, Mother, that's just dust!"

Jay yelled to pull into the Exxon, but with everyone shouting, Brian missed the gas station, tried for a U-turn, missed, and swerved to avoid a head-on with a UPS truck. We went off the road, into a ditch and up again, striking our heads on the ceiling, and plowed to a dead engine halt on a plane of sand.

Everyone jumped out. The opened hood, a broken hose down in there: the power plant seething green bug juice. Brian twisted the radiator cap under a rag, and the geyser of steam sent us all back from the incomprehensible but dying machine.

We all told each other what to do. Everyone disagreed and told someone else to do it instead. Then everybody just did what they wanted to, as if the rest of us could jolly well go to hell. But something was getting done. Jay came back from the Exxon, splashing his khakis with their ten-gallon water can. Brian was standing by the car, taking off his blazer, rolling his sleeves, tucking his tie into his shirt. Heather and I were in the shade of the bull pines, relaxing within whiffing distance of the 7-11's green dumpster, rotten with garbage and flies.

As a family, then, we were placed like statuary around the sandy plane in the center of which sat the dead automobile. A steady breeze of tomatoes and gasoline rippled across the sand. The incidental shadows of birds flitted in patterns and vanished in the harsh brilliance. Only Bubsy stood alone. She walked around her car, dragging her sad little shadow behind her. Her mouth was moving, speaking to the spirits of the family no doubt in the air around her, while with each step her heels sank as though the earth would have her now.

"She's been like this for years." Heather exhaled from her cigarette. "Mom and I are trying to stash her someplace and sell the house, but, Jesus, just mention it and Bubsy freaks."

Our house, I thought. First you steal the beach house, now the city house.

"Bubsy," I shouted, "I'll save you!"

Jay came laughing up the slope as I slid down to save her.

I came abreast of Bubsy and, pacing her, insinuated myself into her arms as though we were dancing in the summery light. Bubsy shook me off. So I grabbed her by the shoulders of her coat and found myself looking into an unrecognizable face. Her life and makeup were melting down her cheeks; she was bewildered. She had gotten old, after all, quite old, and this emergency with the car seemed as far beyond her comprehension as all the times she had played the villain. Her blue eyes, which had reminded me of Bing Crosby only an hour ago, were now lost in exhaustion, and suddenly I saw in them my father's eyes looking at me when he came back with his drink after seeing Great Uncle Howard appear in the dining-room doorway. Bubsy was more than disoriented that moment; she was not in herself, as I gripped her shoulder seams and held us together against the uncertain sand.

"Hey, Bubsy, everything's—Will you look at me?"

She pulled at my hands.

"Bubsy, we're dancing. We're dancing. You like to waltz?"

She began to turn in a little circle.

"Okay? Let's dance. You used to do the Charleston, didn't you? Can you show me?"

She went around and around, under my hand.

Aunt Betty, who had been on the perimeter, now stepped onto the floor of sand. "Mother, please come sit with me."

"Forget it," Heather exhaled, as I came back up the hill. "She didn't even know it was you."

"That was pretty funny, though," Jay said. "Just like Captain Kirk."

"Shut up, Jay. You don't know what you're talking about."

We were silent. Down on the bright disk of sand, under a latent cusp of moon, Aunt Betty and Bubsy were slowly dancing, circling this way and that, leaving traces behind them in the erasable sand. Their voices were sharp, but against the dry roar of traffic in the winter light, the words were indistinct.

"God, I hope they shoot me before I get like that."

"Jeez, Heather," Jay said, "maybe you'll luck out."

"You always were a little smartass, Stuart, or was that Jay?"

"Goddamnit," Brian shouted. "Jay, get over here and give me a hand. I want to get the hell out of here."

And as though I were Jay, I trotted obediently down the hill to help Brian tape up the hose.

III

And then a young waitress was escorting us through an atmosphere chill with air conditioning, past tall French doors, and on to a great round table. Against the vast hush of the empty Yacht Club dining room, we fell into a sort of vesper silence, opened our napkins, and withdrew, each of us, into our own thoughts. Here, by the vast windows, the view was still alive with vivid scenes. Far from returning to the raucous center of my childhood, however, I felt rather as though we had come to the quiet limit of the world. And there was the marble dance floor, black and white in the green turf, where we had baked as sleepy, happy children after swimming, and where, some twenty Labor Days past, the Night Shades had blasted the night away. Where, for one amazing night in their string ties, sharkskin suits, and dark glasses—as the saxophone player blazed a solo while dancing under the limbo stick—for one great party in the wind and the lights, they were cooler than the Beatles. And we were all doing the Peppermint Twist, even Bubsy, the whole family in the music, facing the towers of the city incandescent over a bay of stars.

"So, Brian," Aunt Betty said. "You work for an art gallery. And what do you do, scrub floors?"

"Mo-ther!" Heather rolled her eyes. "Come on, Bubsy, let's take you to the little girl's room. You look like you need a few repairs."

"Look at the weeds," Brian said.

"You could break your neck out there," Jay said. And he was right; the old marble dance floor was breaking apart.

"Oh, you two are such snobs," Aunt Betty giggled. "Well, I'm going to get a salad. They have such a wonderful salad bar."

"Come on, Bubsy, get up. No, you don't need your coat. Look—I have your purse."

When Aunt Betty was gone, Heather said, "I just don't know what makes mother act that way." Then she took Bubsy away.

And it was during this bottomless lull, when all the world seemed to be living elsewhere, that a blonde woman in green slacks appeared in the dining-room doorway. She stood there. Then she came into the room. Heading toward us. I sipped my water. Now almost running, the woman pounced at Brian.

"Do you know that Tom Ogden has been waiting to have lunch with you for the last hour and a half? If you haven't called him yet, you damn well better do it right now."

We bluffed a loud expostulation. "Mom! What the hell are you doing here?"

"Surprise," she said. "I thought I'd pay you a little visit." And her eyebrows pointed almost maniacally.

Aunt Betty was returning from the salad bar. Heather and Bubsy were coming back. Our mother was alone against them—there would be a terrible fight. Mother and Aunt Betty would tear each other apart . . . but our mother was alone. No, she wasn't alone at all. Now in the vaulted entranceway of all those ancient wedding photographs, I saw my other grandmother, Granelle, following on her cane. And she came with reinforcements: our sister Moriah. And I thought, my God, the Ogdens have come to kill the Goodpastures.

And then, in corporeal forms, I saw my gentle Great Uncle Howard in his crisp white yachting cap and Grand Billy limping on his cane, holding a handful of shark's teeth; they were coming toward us, with old Aunts Jule and Amy; and with them, Spiritus Mundi, were two dark, beautiful children, a boy and a girl, whose mother had run away and left them . . .

The actual Aunt Betty stepped behind my mother, encircling her waist to set a salad bowl on the table, and my mother was now turning and, in turning, stepped into Betty's arms.

They took a step together to the right. They said each other's names. They took a step together to the left. They said "hello." And then Aunt Betty stepped back and Mother followed, Aunt Betty turning inward, and Mother turning outward, turning away from us. Then, as I looked again, the far side of the dining room was empty except for a bartender turning a cloth inside a glass while staring at a soap opera on the television. Our mother had come alone after all.

"Carol!" Bubsy called out. She had come back to life. Her face shone with pleasure, as if someone had turned on a light beneath her skin.

"Hello, Lila," and Mother kissed her on the cheek.

Bubsy asked if our father was in town, and the waitress arrived with a large tray of club sandwiches, rich with red tomatoes. And as our mother and Bubsy spoke together, and while Brian was away from the table to call Tom, a sensation of lightness floated up through my mind, as if I were about to faint or become very high. I glanced across the room and stared, then stared hard. My Uncle Andrew stood in the doorway. In fact, his body was across town in a mortuary back room. But, here he stood in this familiar club and looked around at the changes. A busboy who then entered the room excused himself and stepped around my uncle, who moved politely aside. My uncle was at ease, there in his paint-splashed khakis, with his hands in the pockets, and in his old V-neck tennis sweater, which he wore around the porches of our sumer house in Beersheba. He was himself again, as he had been before the cancer. As I continued to stare, his face came around until his eyes met mine, and I had a vision. It was long ago, the summer when I played Powerman, and we were all in the dining room after Rob and Harry had arrived. My grandfather was trying to settle a dispute that had arisen between cousins, something that involved stealing kitchen help. "Forgive them, but don't forget," my grandfather said. And now, as my uncle remained in the dining room doorway, his voice spoke inside my mind while his eyes held me in their gaze. "Forgive them, but don't forget." I smiled over at Bubsy and my mother, without hearing them, and when I looked again, the busboy was at the bar with the bartender. The doorway was empty.

"You got some mayonnaise right . . . here . . . let me get it for you, Bubsy." As my mother had done for her father, Heather now dabbed at Bubsy's cheek. Aunt Betty was signing for the check, and we all pushed our chairs back and rose to our feet.

In the parking lot, I said, "Bye, Bubsy," and hugged her. She giggled like a child overwhelmed by the circus giant. Birds burst from the trees in a chaos of lights and shadows. One of her disks popped, and she screamed a giggle or giggled a scream against my chest.

Jay tapped her on one shoulder, disappeared, then tapped her on the other shoulder and disappeared.

"Knock it off," I said.

"Really," Brian said, but I was unable to guess what his thoughts were or how angry he might still be with Bubsy and all of them.

We gave Heather a lift back to her office. The entire time she did nothing but complain about Bubsy, but all I heard was her bitterness, which until that morning had been my own. We were a tighter family than I had realized, but in relinquishing that inherited rage, I felt as though I could now accept what was left.

We came to a stop. In front on the glass doors a woman was slapping the bare legs of a little boy in shorts and cowboy boots who hopped a lively circle around her, then kicked her in the slats on the do-si-do. The doors flashed multiples of them.

"Well, it was nice seeing you all." Heather got out, then leaned into the window. "Tell Moriah I said 'hello.' And let's try to get together sometime again before we're old and gray."

Well, of course, we said we would. The afternoon was mild, with an ethereal moon disappearing in the winter sky. We didn't say much. We rolled the windows down as we drove away, and some vapor of spring came on the pale warmth. We bumped across the railroad ties. We still had a funeral to attend, but we did not discuss it now. We did not yet know that our father would be there. We slowed down at the red light, which flicked green for us, then turned back into the unending flow of traffic moving around the city along Atlantic Boulevard.

|||||||| Reunions

THE GREETING IN THE AIRPORT DID NOT GO AS BADLY AS HE HAD anticipated. Of course, his father was more embarrassing than usual, but he had expected that. He'd thought ahead of some new, exaggerated characteristic in the old man, some latent lunacy brought out perhaps by the new, if false, landscape of Oklahoma, and had begun to prepare his own deadened respose—to still the muscles in his face—while reading a magazine at thirty thousand feet and descending.

In the long, almost impossibly bright glass corridors beyond the metal detectors—designed to stop terrorists, he noticed, but not zealous, born-again Christians—he was briefly overwhelmed by the families, the husbands and wives and grandchildren reuniting, their voices pitched to the same brilliancy as the light in the glass, and in the midst of so much effusion, he felt his preparations slip just a little.

He saw the old man first—punctual as usual—standing by the baggage claim, both fists at his belt, chin raised. He was scanning the crowd. He still looked small, pot-bellied and handsome with dark hair, but the garish change was obvious. When Brian had last seen his father in an airport—some six months ago in Jacksonville, Florida—the old man had been attired in the conservative Brooks Brothers navy pin stripe of Wall Street, his professional milieu for more than twenty years.

"Son!" His father would have to yell . . . to cup his hands around his mouth. "Son!" He swung both hands up over his head as if he were guiding a plane. "Son!"

The navy suit his father had worn at the family funeral in Jacksonville, which seemed to say he was still normal, had given way now to something Brian had expected, a born-again costume of white shoes, slacks and belt, sky-blue shirt, and sports jacket. A large Celtic cross, garishly gilt and strung on a leather thong, rested on the pale tie. Their handshake was formal, though his father was enthusiastic. Brian felt the square, gold ring on his father's hand as they shook. Otherwise, the greeting had all the usual brio and cheer of a performance, as if the old man hadn't been a broker all his life but an actor in summer stock.

"I was afraid you didn't see me there, boy. And I wouldn't recognize you without your beard. You look decent again. You getting enough sleep?"

"Suitcases aren't down yet?"

"Ah, gee, son, is that all you can say? Let me have a look at you. You look great, boy, just great."

"Dad . . . " Brian pulled back, but went through with it. The hug was brief but tight; the old man's hands embraced him with feeling, then pounded him twice, the signal to let go. It prompted an image he hadn't remembered in years: as a child, cowering in the closet, his father pummeling and kicking at him in a rage over something.

"Well, you're looking well," Brian said.

"Okay, son. Now you better step up there and keep an eye out. Now, step up, son . . . Will you cooperate, please? I don't want anyone to steal your suitcase."

Outside, in the relentless sunshine of the parking lot, Brian slowed to a stop, suitcase in hand, some ten yards away from his father's new vehicle. His father was unlocking the side doors of a large white van with blue signs that read, in white script, TREE OF LIFE MINISTRIES, and was emblazoned further with silver decals of fish, Jesus Christ, and various representations of the cross.

"A little understated, isn't it?"

With great, good cheer, an emotion capable of surrounding any pain with love, his father laughed down at his brilliant shoes, and swung open the side door. "Oh, son, you boys never get tired of ridiculing me, do you?"

They were out in traffic, trying to hit merging speed coming out of the exit ramp.

"We have a truck right on top of us," Brian said. "Can we speed up a little?" And as though the divorce had never happened, or the seven years since then, they were father and son again: Brian, the speed-anxious teenager, his father the cautious conservative. The truck's grid was visible across the back window.

"I'm doing fifty-five as it is, son; now don't badger me. Please, boy —let me think."

Brian squinted at the approaching city in all that sunlight. He hadn't meant for it to start this way, but he had to admit that he felt oddly comfortable. As the muscles of his face relaxed in the warm light, he realized that he couldn't handle being born-agained by his father back in the airport; but here next to him was the real thing from commuterland—the suburban duffer harrassed and out of control, late for the 6:15 into Manhattan or unable to get the lawnmower to operate. This manner of combat was so familiar to them now they didn't know another way. And just as familiar was the old man's gesture—a hand up at the pained temple. Brian turned in his seat.

"Look, Dad, after this car, you've got room on the right—"

"For crying out loud, son, I'm doing the best I can! This thing won't go any faster." His words came halt by painful halt. "Now, son, please . . . I've got . . . a lot on my mind . . . and I can't think about this right now."

Brian cracked his window for a little air and imitated his father's voice: "Well, Goddamnit, son, I guess there won't be any Christmas this year."

He was kidding, but he'd lost his touch; the old man's tolerance had changed on him. In the silence the van accelerated to sixty-five, took one or two abrupt swings to pass slow cars.

"Okay, Dad, you made your point." But his father did not answer; he only accelerated. This was Brian's limit. He would not let his father drag him on; he would not pity him. And as he had done on so many orange, autumnal afternoons during Sunday drives with the whole family squabbling in the car, he retreated into perfect detachment. It had taken adolescent years of practice, but he could still manage it: his father did not move or interest him; he was the silent one. After all, he had been through this before with his father: in all those family outings or evenings around the Christmas tree, the bickering and fighting had brought on scenes between his parents—moments of histrionic insanity so appalling that neither he nor his brothers or sister could believe them later on. The psychologists had certainly found them hard to believe.

The van moderated again in speed. So, maybe the born-again stuff was working; the old man was becoming somewhat tractable. Perhaps the magic had lost a little of its efficacy, though, in the seven years since that night when he received the early evening phone call in his dormitory at Amherst, and his father had announced in one news summary, typical of the broker, that he had left their mother, had accepted Jesus Christ as his lord and savior, was about to marry a wonderful woman, Muriel Wills—a born-again evangelist of renown in Tulsa, Oklahoma—and hoped that Brian would pray for their happiness and, one day, perhaps, love Muriel like a second mother.

"Well, the looney has finally flipped," is how his brothers, Stuart and Jay, and his sister, Moriah, rationalized the desertion. They came back from Davidson's with two bottles of champagne and a few six-packs, and celebrated in the kitchen. "The wicked witch is dead," and they tried to make a roistrous party, but their mother was disconsolate. When the brothers and their sister took turns over the summer staying with her, they all experienced the same thing: waking at 5:00 A.M. to the muffled, half-heard sound of her weeping; and they found the same thing behind many closed doors in the old house—their mother in her nightgown, huddled in the shower behind the closed glass door, weeping so hard into her hands that she had actually begun to wail like an animal. Seven years ago. They had begun talking to the old man again since then. Their mother was not entirely herself yet.

"Ah, gee, son, it's good to see you again. It really is." His father struck him broad-palmed on the knee with good fellowship.

"Well, good to be here. Good to see you again."

But he would not let the old man get to him. Whether his father did or did not believe in all this healing stuff was of no interest or concern to him; he had left that father behind in his college years, just as that father had left his family in fact.

"Mind if we change the station?" Brian said. "I mean, Mozart or something. I'm not into this preacher stuff."

"I'd like you to hear this, son. Give it a chance, open your mind a little. I know—all you East Coast liberals think these guys are crazy. But this one's pretty good. Yale Divinity School." His father slapped him on the knee again. "We've got a lot of things planned for you, son. We've really been looking forward to this."

Brian cracked his window down a bit farther, the wind roaring into his hair, and his father began pointing out buildings of interest in the Tulsa skyline, pale and ethereal in the 11:00 A.M. sunshine of a June morning. And in spite of himself, Brian became interested in what his father had to say.

"Well, here it is, son. What do you think?"

They had stepped out of the elevator onto the eleventh-floor foyer of soapy glass and a pervasive odor of new carpets, fresh paint, and construction dust. His father stood proudly, chest out, fists at belt, and raised his theatrical hand at an office door on which hung a wooden sign, with the carved cursive, TREE OF LIFE MINISTRIES.

"Looks pretty good, Dad. Very impressive."

Inside the office, its three or four rooms seemed to have been occupied not much longer than a week. The undecorated walls of pale paint suspended the summer brilliance throughout the space, making it all somehow seem vast, buoyant, empty, and seeming to flow outside into the open air.

"Candie, I'd like you to meet my second oldest son, Brian." His father clapped him on the shoulders. "He's big Brian, and I'm little Stuart!"

The secretary, prim and erect at her desk, appeared to be assembled from pieces of bright plastic and junk food—from red enamel lips and nails to yellow cotton-candy hair. She laughed joyously with his father, and her tiny gold cross dangled off her rather fullish bosom as she leaned forward to shake his hand with lifeless fingers. Brian reached a magazine off the coffee table and began to flip through it—a local real estate magazine, but still . . .

"Come on, son, take a look around. You can read that later. So, this is it. This is my office and that one's Muriel's. What do you say?"

How had his father come to this? The old Manhattan office came up in this mind with all its sensations of warm darkness, Persian carpets, and Queen Anne furniture, the Flemish landscapes on the walls. That was gone. He now stood now amid three empty rooms of toneless radiance. On one door hung a wooden sign with his father's name and title, CHAIRMAN AND PRESIDENT. At the other end of the coffee table, the open door revealed an office empty but for sunlight and a telephone that sat on the carpet; the sign read, MURIEL WILLS, SENIOR EXECUTIVE VICE PRESIDENT. His father's window gave a view of the city's rational grid of streets, Muriel's one of rolling pasture land with oil derricks like spikes pressing into the sky.

"Well, looks great. Really does," Brian said, and was aware of falling into the false tone of praise that his father had always used on him when he was growing up—when his father didn't want to be bothered, which was always. "Really does, Dad. Just wonderful. Very impressive."

His father looked at his shoes and seemed to be sorting car keys from change in his pocket. "Well, we've just moved in, son," he said. "Wait 'til we really get it set up."

"Amen," Candie said. "Oh, he's so much like you. He's so cute, your son!"

His father laughed, struck him warmly across the back and shoulder. Brian laughed with them and casually leaned over to pick up the magazine again. "Oh, he sure is, isn't he? Just a chip off the old block!"

Five minutes later, in his father's office, door closed, they were into it.

"Son, I'd like you to sign these before we meet Muriel. It's very important to us. We have a lot of people counting on us."

"How about a prospectus first. Something I can read."

"Son, will you please put that down and give me a minute here?"

With a pang, as though he were a high school senior again, Brian sat up and crossed his legs conservatively. "I thought I made it clear I haven't decided yet."

"Didn't you get the letter I sent you?"

"We all read it. But what's the big secret? Why don't you just tell us—"

"It's insured, son. You'll get it all back. I'm trying to make things up for you and everyone else, and your mother, don't you see that?"

"I still don't see where the money's going to come from."

"Oh, God, son, didn't Stuart or Jay tell you that? It's part of Bubsy's estate. She's agreed to let each of you liquidate your share but only for this project. That's all that's left over from the orange grove trust fund."

"What project?" He flipped the magazine open.

"Will you just trust me, son? I know what I'm doing. I will triple your money by Christmas."

"Look, Dad, if it's such a sure deal, why don't you just show me some contracts, a list of investors, or banks, or someone else I can discuss this with? You can't expect me to just sign over my inheritance like that. Come on. And what does that mean? That you're going to put Bubsy into a nursing home? Then who gets her house? I just saw Heather when we were down there, and she says they're going to sell it. So, where does that leave us? First, the orange grove, then the warehouse, the beach house, Bubsy's house, and now our inheritance? No, no, no." He shut the magazine and looked up. "Are you listening to me?"

Hand over the eyes, face down, his father was muttering at the green desk blotter, the gold-ringed hand closed in a fist.

Brian sat back and crossed his legs the other way. He glanced across a shelf of family pictures, most from almost a decade ago, and began to stare at a stand-up table frame that contained a photograph of them all around the baby grand piano. Christmas, high school, terrible fighting, the pose as a family, all those practiced smiles. Outside the streaked glass, from this angle in his canvas deck chair, the pattern of streets blended into the range of pastures and oil derricks. His father was still muttering. Brian leaned forward, elbows on knees.

"Dad . . . Dad? I don't speak Russian . . . or whatever you're . . . "

Shocked, Brian stood up out of the chair, crossed the room, and closed the door behind him as if he'd been witness to something private and obscene.

"Is your father still in conference now?" Candie smiled and tilted her head. She had one hand over the receiver. "It's Muriel, line four."

"Put her through. They can speak in tongues together." And he smiled back at her with Christian sweetness as he went into the hallway.

In the twilight of 6:30, when the Oklahoma sky was warm with summer and blending pale shades of green over the city, he and his father left the condo where they had showered, changed, and watched the local news together—two men of taller-than-average height crossing a mundane parking lot to a white van. They drove out on the highway to meet Muriel for dinner.

"Isn't there a Chinese joint anywhere in this city?"

"Oh, son, won't you bend even a little?"

On a strip of shopping malls with crimson and turquoise traffic lights glaring beautifully in the dusk, they met Muriel at a Roy Rogers. They stepped out of the van and he saw her. In these crowds there was no one else who could be her. People were going through the doors, but Muriel had to be the woman who was alone at the side of the building. She stood between the low boxwoods, her eyes closed and both her palms pressed against the dark bricks. Brian recognized the blonde hair, the figure. As she leaned more forcefully against the wall, her profile came into view beneath her arm. Her eyes were closed; her lips were speaking words.

"I'm sorry, but I cannot . . . I can't . . . I can't do this."

"Oh, I know, son. We all embarrass you so much."

"What is she doing—healing the restaurant?"

His father slapped him lightly on the shoulder. "Well, it must be working, son. We've never gotten sick here."

As they approached her—and this was going just as he might have guessed—Brian noticed that no one but him seemed to pay Muriel much attention. Her mouth was working, her hands moving over the surface of bricks. Men opened the doors for their children and ushered them inside, but no one stared at Muriel; only the children did, and their mothers turned them away. And that was it, as if the healing of buildings were a commonplace.

Brian stood at the counter, submerged in reading the billboard menu, when he heard their voices among the others at the opening doors. He had only just turned around when Muriel squeezed him in a full embrace. Her arms went around his back. Her cheek was on his chest. Her breasts pushed fat against his stomach. His arms were pinned beneath hers. He hardly got a word out, though when she drew away from him, he saw what a pretty woman she was in spite of the makeup and the rosin of blonde in her brownish hair.

"Oh, hi—good to see you." He nodded awkwardly, put his hands in his pockets. "So—are the cheeseburgers here any good?"

"Oh, Muriel, you'll have to forgive him. He's still an easterner, and I'm afraid we embarrass him a little."

"I prayed to Jesus to bring your plane here safely."

Brian turned to her. "Well, I'm sure the air traffic controllers and I are indebted. Now, if God would only make some money for us."

"Son—"

"Oh!" She shoved Brian lightly in the shoulder. "You haven't changed!" And she laughed.

Brian felt the blush. He would not stoop to mockery, like Jay or Stuart. He withdrew into his chill disinterest, but as they talked of other things he thought, so what? And he warmed to Muriel—a bosomy flirt in fuck-me heels, a pink, figure-gripping jumpsuit of nubby cotton, and a gold cross—as he might have warmed to an Elvis impersonator. There was no harm, really.

"You look wonderful, Muriel," he said, sliding into his bucket seat at a window table. "Been awhile, hasn't it?"

Now, with eyes closed, Muriel raised her hands into the air beside her head and began to chatter in tongues over their trays of burgers, cokes, and fries. Brian leaned back and crossed his legs at the knee. He draped one arm over the back of the next seat. He wore a public smile and looked about to establish some bond of sympathy, but again no one was looking at them. His eyes met those of an old woman in the corner; she frowned at him, then bit into her chicken leg. And that was it. None of this was what he had expected.

The first time he and his brothers had met Muriel, five weeks ago after the funeral of his Uncle Andrew in Jacksonville, their father had taken them out to a Mexican restaurant for dinner. After they had ordered, Muriel announced to the whole table that she wanted to tell them a little story. The story lapsed into twenty minutes, then forty, and finally revealed itself to be a full-scale witnessing of the divinity of Jesus Christ. For over an hour, Muriel besieged them all—sweetly and ferociously—trying to convert them at the table.

"And I saved the man in the hospital, when I had a vision of Christ that told me to go and see him. I came into his room in the hospital and he looked at me like I had forty heads and forty arms and forty legs—"

Stuart Jr., droll, interrupted. "That was *his* vision, Muriel."

General shouting.

By then the dinner had become a trench war. Brian and his brothers flung conversational hand grenades at Muriel and his father; their older sister argued theology; and it all ended in accusations, flung-back chairs, and storming exits. Another godawful scene with the lunatic Goodpastures.

"So, tell me about your job, Brian," Muriel said. "Your father is so proud of you, working on the Hill. And your sister is now a lawyer, and Jay is in a rock band, and Stuart—"

"Still finding himself," his father said. "I hope he gets with it soon—meets a nice girl and finds a career for himself. But Brian here is working in the Senator's office."

"I know," Muriel said. "And it sounds so exciting. Especially to us —way out here."

No witnessing, not a word about Jesus.

While Muriel was in the "little girls' room," Brian and his father sat in silence. His eyes fell on his father's hand. "See you still got that ring Mom made you. Can I see it?"

His father dropped the ring into his palm. Brian turned it over—a heavy gold ring with his father's initials raised on a square boss. His mother had made it in an art class back when they were both grad students and engaged. He palmed the ring; it was heavy, too tight for his own fingers. His father might have a new life, but he still held onto artifacts of the old one. "Here." Brian handed it back as Muriel plopped down, fresh and invigorated.

"So, did you and your father have a chance to talk about the investment? We're hoping to break ground in December."

"Break ground?" Brian looked at his father, who did not look back.

Muriel sucked vanilla shake through the straw. "For the new children's wing of the Oral Roberts University hospital."

"I thought his name was Anal Roberts."

Muriel turned the straw in her shake. His father glanced at him, then out the window again.

"I'm sorry," Brian said. "That was uncalled for. What is this, a children's wing of a hospital? I'm still not clear on all the details."

Muriel filled him in, and, as if she were witnessing, the answer evolved into an elaborate twenty-five minute precis of stocks for investors, returns, insurance, the names of banks and builders, contractors, architects, and city councilmen. She even prompted Brian's memory of a downtown construction site they'd passed, telling him that the three-hundred-bed unit, specializing in burns and cancer treatment, would be nondenominational. His father drank his coffee as if he were far away—or had heard all this a million times—and Brian recognized in Muriel's outline the strategems of his father, veteran of Korea and Merrill Lynch. All of it just fine, if perhaps a little too well worked out.

"That's interesting." Brian sat back. "But before I sign anything, I'll have to call Moriah. Stuart and Jay and Moriah. Talk to them."

"Oh, they've already signed," Muriel said. "They gave your father power of attorney yesterday."

Brian looked at his father, who was gazing out the window. "Why didn't you tell me this?"

His father now looked at him. "I didn't want to prejudice you, son. You're the last one."

Brian flipped a french fry at his plate. Outside the window, beyond the reflections of themselves at the table, headlights were gliding through the darkness of the parking lot. "I still have to think it over."

Muriel placed her hand on his father's knee. "It's almost nine-thirty, if we want to catch the movie."

And after the movie and before bed she said not a word about money or church or Jesus. She did not pray in public or heal the theater. And as they walked ahead of him beneath the street lights, back toward the condo, he could not help but notice how normal they were together.

11

After seven days Brian signed the papers that gave his father power of attorney over his $60,000 share of his grandmother's estate. He did not sign because he was forced to but because he wanted to, though in

the months that followed he would find his reasons increasingly diffi-
cult to explain to others, much less to himself.

Perhaps—he later told himself—perhaps he signed because no one
had asked him to after that first night. For the duration of that first
week, and he was there for ten days out of the office, neither his father
nor Muriel bothered him. They did not discuss religion. In fact, it was
Brian who brought it up whenever they went out for dinner.

"No, seriously, Muriel, just tell me . . . How does God talk to you?
You hear voices, visions?"

"Because I know Him and I know what He wants me to do."

"But what if it's just a little devil pretending to be Jesus? How can
you tell? I'm serious. How do you tell?"

"Son, please—"

"I have Christ in my heart and He speaks to me there."

"So, 'faith' is what you're saying—"

"'Trust in the Lord with all thine heart,'" she said, "'and lean not
unto thine own understanding.' Psalms."

"But Muriel . . . Dad, will you please just— Muriel, how can you
believe in anything if you haven't believed in nothing yet? Where do
you make the leap, and why?"

"Are you saying you don't believe in God? Then who made the uni-
verse? Who made the big bang?"

"Got you there, son." His father laughed.

Brian stirred his coffee. "I'm not arrogant enough to say He doesn't
exist, but I am arrogant enough to ask."

"Well, if you knew Jesus, you wouldn't have to ask."

"But that's . . . that's like shutting off your mind. Why do we have
to—" Brian tossed another french fry onto his tray. "Is she praying for
me? Goddamnit, Dad, tell her to knock it off, will you?"

"She doesn't want you to go to hell, son. And neither do I. It would
break your mother's heart."

In the mornings he and his father didn't talk much. Almost until
the moment she walked out the door, Muriel strolled around the
condo in a loosely tied pink satin robe which allowed a glancing but
generous view of her heavy breasts. "Why don't you come in and join
us," his father would call from the breakfast nook. "What's the matter,
son, you afraid to look at us?" And Brian would get off the sofa, shut
off the TV, and join them at the table bright with eastern windows.

But he could not sit and listen to their cooing, their little daily plans and occasional praise of Jesus—a life of emotional reassurance that his mother had never known. Brian returned to the warm, dark living room and turned on the TV. His father's smile was pointed, however, as if to say that he knew what this was really about, and Brian found himself irritated into a cold and embarrassed silence.

After Muriel had gone for the day, however, he and his father got along surprisingly well. In the absence of siblings, the old marriage, and other pressures, they eased into a style of relaxed and combative conversation, and their targets were not each other but corruptions in the world. They watched the news and decried nuclear power, terrorists, and Reagan—which Brian considered a leap for the man who had voted for Goldwater and Nixon when he was still naive enough to vote. When whole afternoons went by without any tension behind the silence, Brian began to feel as though he and his father were housemates of different generations. And why not? In Washington he worked with men his father's age in the Senator's office. After lunch their partings were amicable. He would be out by the pool, reading. His father would stop to tell him he was going to a business meeting. "Dressed like that?" Brian said. "Who would take you seriously?"

"Oh, you boys really love to shoot me down," his father said, but the tone was one of light self-mockery. They both got a laugh out of it.

"Well, I don't like it," Muriel said one night in the kitchen. "He's going to make us all look bad."

"You don't understand, Muriel," his father said.

Brian came in from the living room, where he'd been watching the national news. Muriel told him they were talking about Hayes Johnson, a local oil man who was on the verge of becoming big time in religion.

"Oh, Hayes has this donation thing," Muriel said. "Some deal. He gets a $10,000 tax write-off or donation for every new convert, and the person who saves him gets ten percent."

Brian smiled broadly. "Really? How interesting. You mean, he's a headhunter for Christ? Or would you call him a bounty-hunter?" He laughed out loud.

Muriel turned on his father. "You see? You think he's any different? They'll all say that!"

"You don't understand, Muriel." His father got up and opened a cabinet door, looking for something not at hand. "Jesus, help her to understand." He laughed a little.

"What my father means, Muriel—whenever he says, 'you don't understand'—is that he has to do this, no matter how stupid it is, because he has to do something that'll hurt you and destroy himself. Dear old dad is a bit of a masochist."

"You laugh," Muriel said to his father, "but he's right."

His father said, "Satan, in Jesus' name, I command you to get behind me. Leave them in peace."

"I'm sorry, but I don't think that's funny." Muriel went into the living room, then down the hall.

"Oh, come on," Brian called out, "lighten up, Muriel. He's just kidding." The door of the master bedroom shut. Brian was about to ask his father if he really believed all this stuff, or why he bothered to marry Muriel or deal with all these zealots. But as he turned, he saw his father, not an old man but an oldish one, standing by the refrigerator with his eyes closed, lips moving in silent prayer. Brian went back out to the television.

One afternoon his father took him to a clothing store, ostensibly to buy a tie for himself, but started pressuring him to try on a few jackets. Brian refused, arguing that he bought his own clothes now, but his father manipulated the born-again salesman into helping him, and to Brian's amusement he found himself standing in front of the mirrors in a pale blue searsucker suit, like his father's, having the trousers chalked and pinned. "Please Jesus, give my son some taste in men's clothing." It was all very droll and full of inside jokes, but the salesman didn't catch on, and so it seemed even funnier that somehow the purchase of an ordinary searsucker suit—which he would need in D.C. anyway for the summer heat—was treated at the cash register like a conversion. He was given a receipt and a "Praise Jesus." Then, out in traffic, his father of the old suburban days began to fulminate at other drivers.

"God forgive you," Brian said. He began to pray in tongues. "Folderol ad nauseaum, embezzlementum, Ahhaaa-men."

His father slapped him on the thigh. "Ah, son, it's good to have you around again. You keep me honest."

Brian looked out the window at the traffic. "Can we change the station?" he said, and as his father relented, tuning in a jazz station, Brian realized that he was enjoying himself.

And yet, sometimes when they went out for dinner at the Burger King, no one sat near them.

"Your father has been teaching me everything in the world about business. And you know, he is so modest!"

"Well, he has a lot to be modest about. Don't you, Dad?"

Muriel patted his father's fist, on the ring. She looked at it for a moment.

Brian forked up a fry. "He ever tell you about the time he tried to sacrifice me? What was I, Dad, five, six? 'Son,' he said, 'if you're ever about to be run over by a train, lie down between the rails.' And while we're standing in this empty train station, he makes me lie down between the rails. Just like that. I'm lying there on the ties, on the rocks, the rails right next to my head. Lucky thing it was a local line and Saturday. Or, you know—and, hey, it was probably the hand of God that stayed him, hunh, Dad?"

His father looked at his hands. "He's making it up, Muriel; it never happened. I never did such a thing."

"Right there in the middle of this empty commuter station. Saturday afternoon. I'm lying down between the rails, with weeds scratching my ears, the sun in my face. 'Son, you don't understand. I have to do this.' Can you imagine?"

His father laughed. "Are you trying to tell me it didn't build character, son?"

"Oh! Okay, how about this one . . . " They appeared to stop listening mid-anecdote, so he dropped it.

"Oh, son, now I wish I had fought for custody. Your mother has warped you all so. Told you stories. Turned you against me. Made you hate me."

"We learned it all from you, Elmer Gantry."

"Is that your opinion of me, son, that I'm evil? That's a little sophomoric, don't you think? I would've hoped you'd be beyond that by now, smart boy like you. You even went to college."

"Oh, I know—U.Va.," Muriel was saying. "We're all so impressed."

Brian could not control the stridency of his voice. "You like to laugh it off, but you get sacrificed sometime, see how you like it. Come on, Dad, count 'em up." Brian splayed his fingers to tap on each one. "Orange groves, warehouse, Bubsy, Brian, Mom, Jay . . . and, hey, how about the beatings or the belt buckle? You tell her about that? Did he, Muriel? Come on, man, be honest. Jesus loves you, right? I mean, you planted the oak, so what if it falls and kills you?"

His father laughed, the old surburban dad. "Well, this is fascinating, son, but why don't we pursue this another time, when we've all had too much to drink?"

Brian put his chin in his palm and glared into the parking lot. Headlights were gliding in the dark. Then he laughed.

"You're not being fair," Muriel said.

He and his father both looked at her.

"Well, son, I know I did some terrible things, and I just hope you can forgive me some day. But I was full of hatred then, filled with Satan, and your mother was no support—"

Brian would not let himself say another word; he wanted to, but he had already said much more than he was aware of even remembering. Muriel laid one hand over his father's fist, then pulled his hand away from his chin. She made a compound of their grouped hands at the center of the table.

"Now, let's all go to a movie. And stop this quarrelling. 'Cause if you don't, I'll pray for us all right here."

She was kidding, but Brian had lost his touch. He was the first one outside in the summer darkness of the parking lot. And yet, wasn't he overreacting?

When they came home after the movie, he and his father became remote. Muriel swished through the condo in her loose satin robe. Every time she swung her glass of cranberry juice to make a point about the children's hospital—to his father in the breakfast nook, to him in the living room—the lapels would blouse open, revealing her heavy breasts down to the nipples, which made points in the satin. There she stood in the semi-darkness talking to them both, this frowzy bottle-blonde with a burned-out, baby-doll look, cute nose, and pouty lower lip. He began to see her as his father's kept woman, his personal and salacious Marilyn Monroe.

So that was behind the conversion. His father wasn't just born again; he was laid again. Brian felt ashamed and sorry for his mother on these evenings, when he refused to look at Muriel. His station wagon–driving, bake sale–organizing, hospital-volunteering, Republican mother had become mannish with age and respectability and the sexless clothing of a Maine catalog. In spite of all his filial feelings, he could not exactly blame his father.

Brian began to anticipate Muriel's runs to the kitchen. He would sit in the lights of a late-night talk show, palming a can of cold beer. Around midnight, after an hour in the bedroom, she would come sashaying down the hallway and into the flickering living room. She chucked ice cubes in two glasses and uncapped the tonic water, lapels blousing, her breasts spilling into the dimness. She would talk to him, nothing much, but the tone of her voice and her air of disheveled wantonness permeated the room like a musk of after-sex. He knew she was performing. She had to know what she was doing. And worse, one night, when she asked him gently if he wanted the TV off—he had begun to drowse—he looked up at her in her loose robe, with her full calves and full smile all underlit—holding two drinks as if one were for him—and he knew that if he met her in a bar, he would go for it. "No," he said curtly, and sat up. She walked down the hall, quickly, and he hoped she had caught the insult in his tone.

He and Muriel still argued whenever they went out for dinner.

"Satanism is on the rise," she said one night in a McDonald's.

"Since the Middle Ages?" Brian said. "Hard to believe."

"What about all those reports?" she said.

"What reports?"

"That rock band, Kiss—Knights in Satan's Service—and all those kids playing Dungeons and Dragons."

"That's not Satanism," Brian said. "That's the suburbs. It's called juvenile delinquency. Some day they'll be tax attorneys."

"Well, then," Muriel smiled at him. "I see we agree."

Brian blanched, which prompted him and Muriel to laugh together. But then he met his father's smile and blushed with sharp, itching heat, as if he were a boy again and his father had caught him masturbating in the bathroom. His father had a genius for making the expression of every emotion feel like a humiliation—and so the falsity, the good cheer. But as he and his brothers grew up, loathing him, they learned to play the old man's game, however false; for, after all, when it was well used, it was a rhetoric as connotative and playful as any other, and one that took considerable acuity to play well.

"Ah, look," his father said. "He's blushing, Muriel. Isn't that cute?"

Brian's glance was cold reproval, but he could see Muriel looking at him, as if she thought it was more than cute. He decided that was only because he had taken her side in that fight about Hayes Johnson.

Had his father been easygoing like this when he was growing up? Not at all. When had his father ever been relaxed and full of conversation in the mornings and evenings? Never. Brian decided he was wrong to condemn his father's new life. Wasn't his father, after all, just as entitled to practice the rituals of his cult as the Hassidim of Brooklyn or the Voodoo of Miami? And wasn't that his objection, really— embarrassment?

No, his father was entitled to this world. His father had grown up in the shadows of western decline to become its last acute manifestation—the Ivy League Man—and this new spiritual plateau offered him respite and solace, a chance to deny his failures as father, son, and businessman. He had carried those failures for some thirty years; they had imploded, exploded into divorce; and here he was piecing the fragments of himself back into a passable composite—the Wall Street executive, the well-read man, the man of God.

One morning at the start of the second week, just before he signed the papers, Brian realized that he would always be his father's son as long as he acted like a brat and tried to exact punishment for wounds that were now fifteen years old—wounds that were old enough now to be in high school themselves. He no longer played with skateboards or Stingray bikes, so perhaps it was time to box a few of his pet hatreds for the Salvation Army.

That morning, without being called, he joined them in the breakfast nook. "So, what's on the agenda for today?" he said, and went on to speak of things that interested them, saying that he wanted to meet their friends, even attend a prayer meeting. In the eastern sunlight of the windows, he saw his father then as he might have seen an older man in his office—lines in his face and exhaustion under his eyes, a facade of accomplishment hiding a background of failures. There were men in his office like this; did their sons feel as he did? He got up for more coffee, prompted by a sensation of love for his father. All of his rationalizations about having come out here for a vacation disappeared. All his bullying looked to him now like the behavior of a child nagging for attention. The past was only a landscape buried beneath the present, and on this new terrain, he was willing to meet his father like any other adult male, to learn his mind and forget what lay between and beneath them.

He poured coffee at the stove. Muriel was chatting away, and he was glad—she preserved the old man, and kept the moment going forward. For no reason he could understand clearly, he felt like he would cry, for his father and all the stupid, hateful things that had separated them. "I always wished I had been friends with my father," the old man had once told him. Brian could break the pattern. It was natural, of course. All he really wanted to do was love him. He blinked his eyes back under control. The absurd swelling receded from his throat. "Hey, there's no cream," he called. Then he sat with them again by the windows, where they all talked about their plans for the next few years.

III

The heavy sunshine of high afternoon filled his father's office with a drowsy warmth. The door latch clicked and Candie came in, excusing herself for waking Brian from his momentary nap.

"Not yet, hunh?" he said.

"I don't know where they could be," Candie said. "But, you know, you might want to go ahead without them. Ivy Green, just around the corner? Has a wonderful salad bar."

"Not even a message?"

She opened a loaded file drawer in a steel cabinet. "All I know is they want that geologist's report. Your father didn't say where it was, did he?" She shut the drawer, opened the one above. She fanned the tops of files, then spoke loudly enough to be heard in the waiting room. "Just a minute!"

Brian took his ankles off the desk; he sat up. A large man with big white hair and a blue suit had walked across the space of the waiting room to the doorway.

"Here we go!" Candie slipped a manila folder up out of a file. The large man came through the doorway into his father's office. Candie handed him the report, then kept scanning files. Brian stood up behind the desk. The man read the papers with evident satisfaction, then stepped toward the desk. He extended his hand.

"Well, congratulations," he said. "You must be 'little' Brian. Hayes

Johnson. Your father has told me so much about you. Washington sounds wonderful." He laughed pleasantly. His handshake conveyed the deep, overpowering love of his sect but also had just a touch of the business crush. "I haven't met a young millionaire before. Congratulations, Brian."

"Ah!" Candie said. "That's why. These two are stuck . . . just a little . . . " She peeled two blueprint sheets carefully apart. "I really know He will show her today, Mr. Johnson." Candie handed him the sheet. "I can really feel it. I mean, with all the wells in Tulsa, how could He miss?"

The two of them laughed pleasantly. Mr. Johnson's voice was deep and reassuring. "Well, praise Jesus is all I can say. Just praise Him, every day."

"Amen. You know, I just love Him so much!" Candie crossed her arms and squeezed herself.

"You and your brothers are very lucky to have the father you do." Hayes Johnson turned on Brian. His eyes were large, direct, and peaceful; they conveyed a soft but overwhelming confrontation, one that allowed no way around him. The Celtic cross that lay upon his tie caught the light. "Now, of course, we haven't had the luck we'd hoped for . . . "

"Mmmm." Candie frowned at the carpet, hugging herself.

"But we're not counting dry wells today. What is it, four, five? I don't even know." He and Candie laughed joyously. "But today, I think we'll do it. I know it. I can feel His love flowing over me, can't you, Candie? Will you join me in prayer? Will you, Brian? Please, come forward, and join us."

To shake hands, Brian had already come around the desk, but he knew Hayes would pretend otherwise, that he would say later Brian had joined them in prayer. He folded his arms. Mr. Johnson and Candie closed their eyes, lowered their faces, and clasped their hands below their waists.

"Lord," Mr. Johnson said, "we ask you today to forgive us, to take our lives and show us your will. Lord, we ask you to guide Muriel today while she stands out there with those geologists and those men running the drilling equipment. We ask you to make her wise, to make her eyes see and her foot not to step falsely. We ask that you give her strength against these men of science who do not know your

world, that she might work a miracle today in your name only, for
your glory that these men shall see you are the one God, the light and
the way forever. In Jesus' name we pray. Amen."

"Amen," Candie said.

Their faces came up curiously drained and beatific with pleasure.

"Uh, excuse me," Brian said. "Let me get this clear. Dad and Muriel
are drilling for oil?" He snorted a laugh. "That doesn't . . . I mean, I'm
not sure, uh . . . "

Hayes Johnson had come over to him, overwhelming him with his
enormous size, backing him over the desk. He crushed Brian's shoulders between his large hands as though Brian were a huge tube of
toothpaste and his rational mind could be popped off. Mr. Johnson's
face came close to his: big, pink, and shaved. And as he raised his
closed eyes and began to speak to the light fixtures, he gave off a whiff
of lemon-lime after shave. He then placed his broad and encompassing
hand over Brian's brow and palmed his forehead. "Jesus, in your name
I ask you to heal this one, to take away his doubts and confusion. Jesus, I ask you to take away his pain and give him peace of understanding that his doubts may not affect Muriel today when she chooses the
next site for a miracle to praise your eternal glory, Amen."

"Amen," Candie said.

Released, Brian could not speak. He had been healed. The sensation
in his legs and arms was one of drowsy peacefulness, slightly bizarre
and alien, not at all scary but quite relaxing, actually, as if he'd had a
deep massage; and though he distantly recognized this as the effect of
love-bombing—so called in the press—he had never felt its sensual,
almost narcotic pleasure. A small voice went through the back of his
mind, saying, "Do it again, Do it again"; and as he looked at Candie,
pretty, breasty, and available, the vague notion of seducing her in the
empty afternoon office crossed his mind as a wonderful ambition. For
a moment he was outside and above himself, watching Candie and Mr.
Johnson walk into the waiting room and also regretting that he had
signed any papers at all. When he landed on his intellectual feet a moment later, the door was closed and he was standing amid canvas deck
chairs in the sunshine of an almost empty office.

The file drawers were locked. Had she turned a key? He hadn't been
watching that closely. The drawers of his father's desk were also
locked. He stood at the window, looking at the grid of streets. He

went into the waiting room. Candie, now alone, sat at the reception desk, typing a letter slowly and watching her fingers.

Brian picked up the real estate magazine. "Well, I guess they'll be some time. Which bank was it that they were going to again?"

Candie hit back space, then rolled the paper up to check the erasure. She lifted a bottle of Wite-Out, gave it a shake.

"I'm really not sure." She laid down a careful stroke of the brush.

"Five dry wells." Brian flipped back and forth through the magazine, noticing now that it had pictures of pastures and oil derricks. "What did the geologists' report say, Candie?"

"They are men of science." She blew on the page. "They do not know His world."

"Well, that's true," Brian said. "But what did they say?"

"You'll have to ask your father and Muriel. I really don't know."

"You, uh, just work here," he said.

She rolled the paper down and began to type slowly again.

"Well, praise Jesus," Brian said.

Candie's sweet southern accent began to flatten out. "Look, I had nothing to do with any of this. You want to know, ask your father."

Brian turned a page in the magazine. "Well, I will, I guess, later on. But you keep a list of their appointments, right? You're the, uh, office manager. You do that?"

"It could be dozens of banks they're at. All I know is they're going out." She shut off the typewriter.

"Okay, fine. Then where's the drill site? If I'm going to be an investor, I get to see it, don't I?"

She locked the letter in her top drawer, shouldering her purse as she came around the desk. "Look, I think you have a lot to talk about with your father. And all I know is he'll be home because there's a prayer meeting at Mr. Johnson's tonight. So you can just leave me out of it." She closed the door hard behind her.

"Well, praise Jesus," Brian said, and thrashed the magazine against the wall. He saw himself smashing all the plants, knocking chairs everywhere, but didn't. Instead, he kicked the magazine into Muriel's barren office. The view through her windows was one of rolling pastures and oil derricks.

He spent the afternoon telephoning city banks around Tulsa, but not a secretary had heard of Tree of Life Ministries, or understood his reason for calling. "What miniseries?" one of them said. He telephoned his brothers and sister but could not reach them. He paced about the condo, fulminating, though by twilight he had grown quiet. In the foyer the door opened. He could hear his father set down his briefcase. Brian walked out, smiling.

"Ah, there he is. So, what's up? Anything new?"

"Didn't you get my message? About tonight, son. I want you to meet Hayes Johnson. You said you wanted to go to a prayer meeting; here's your chance. Now, come on. We have forty-five minutes and you're not even showered. I can smell you from here."

"Well, guess what, Dad? I did meet him—when he came by to get the geologists' report today. Let's clear this up real easy, okay, Dad? Dad, are you listening to me? We gave you—no, we lent you—that money for a children's hospital, not an oil well, right? You didn't use it to drill for oil, right?"

His father laughed, and without looking at him, walked into the bedroom, loosening his tie. "Oh, son, still trying to shoot me down? And just when I thought you'd begun to outgrow that sort of thing."

Brian went after him down the hall. "Dad—"

"Son, do you honestly think we don't have more than one investment going on at a time?" he called from inside the dressing closet. "What do you take me for? What kind of corporation would this be if we weren't diversified?"

"Great. Fantastic. Glad to be a part of it, Dad. So show me that prospectus. Wasn't ready a week ago. No, Candie had to type it. Well, okay. Let's go." He felt the muscles go tight through his shoulders. "Because if you and Muriel are into some crackpot scheme—Oil Wells from God—we will get a lawyer and we will fucking crush you."

"Oh, son, it pains me to hear you talk like that. Please, Jesus, heal his pain. My son is in pain."

"Just tell me. Did you put it in the wells or the hospital?"

His father had closed the bathroom door and turned on the shower. "Which one what, son? You have to speak up. I can't hear you."

Brian opened the door, put a hand onto his father's chest, and shoved him back into the towel rack. "Now," he said, "let's go over this carefully, just to make sure—"

"I have to answer the phone, son."

"I want to see contracts, financial statements—"

"Goddamnit, boy, get out of my way!"

"Dad," Brian lowered his voice, "let go of my hands, okay? All we have to do is talk about this, like business, okay—"

"That may be the bank!"

Brian released him, then went down the hallway after him. In the living room his father was speaking into the phone with the calm baritone assurance of an old-time radio announcer, but in the afterlight of day, wearing a cheap brown bathrobe, the old man looked pathetic. The familiar tone of self pity had begun to undermine the confident baritone.

"Well, if it's all right with you, I'd like to keep this conversation open another week just to investigate all our options. Right. Well, I'm sorry, too. I'll get back to you, though. Good enough. Right."

His father set down the receiver, stood motionless, then kneeled. "Jesus," he said, "what have I done to offend you?" He went on a moment in tongues, then abruptly stood up. Brian backed away from him.

"Goddamn bastards," the old businessman muttered. "Don't talk to me now, boy. You'll get your money back. All of it. I'll pay all you bastards back, even if I have to kill myself for the insurance. Would that satisfy you, to have me dead? I don't have a goddamn cent to my name. I can't make payments on the mortgage or the car or the office. I'm strapped up to here, boy. It's all I can do to keep Jay in college—"

"He graduated two years ago and Mom paid for that."

"Well, don't believe everything your mother says. She's not right in the head."

"That's what she says about you. She says you're a scheming, dishonest—"

"All right! Jesus Christ, boy, give it a rest! You want to believe her just because she's your mother, you go right ahead. It's goddamn sentimental and intellectually dishonest. I thought you were smarter than that, but I don't give a goddamn any more. I don't give a goddamn about anything any more. You can all go to hell!" He slammed the door, but his voice could still be heard talking in the bedroom. "Forgive me, Jesus. God almighty, take my life and show me the way."

Brian followed him down the hall into the bedroom and pushed open the bathroom door. The shower curtain was moving. "Okay, fine, Dad. But let's just be reasonable. We'll clear this all up, then I can leave tomorrow, and things'll be fine, just the way they were, okay?"

The curtain snapped back. His father's face was bloated, soaking. "What do you know about it, boy? Sometimes we pray and the next day a thousand dollars arrives in the mail." The curtain snapped back.

"But, Dad, that's like a chain letter. That's not faith. That's . . . I don't know . . . organizing or something." His father shouted at him now to get out of the bathroom, so he did, vaguely aware that the front door of the condo had opened and shut. "God, what a moron I am. You really got me good, man! I really fell for it this time."

Muriel's purse landed on the bed. Brian turned. She was swinging her jacket off, strong, in control. "I spoke to Hayes," she yelled through the bathroom door. She kicked her high heels into the dressing closet. "He said 'Yes.' For the first quarter. Stuart, did you hear me? We can sign tonight, after the prayer meeting. Oh, thank you, Jesus." She looked at Brian. "Little miracle never hurt anyone."

He was conscious of standing alone with her in a darkened bedroom. He could feel her watching him begin to blush. "I worry so much when your father gets like this. I mean . . . I cannot take this much longer. Someday I'll show you the notes I've found."

Muriel held onto his arm as if to reassure him, then balancing herself, her breast against his arm, she lowered her head down to the level of his belt as she slipped a stocking down her leg. "Don't worry." She came back up. "I was with Hayes all afternoon, while your father was at the bank. God, the things I do. Now get dressed. We're late as it is."

"He's 'big Brian,' and I'm 'little Stuart!'"

Everyone in the living room laughed at the joke, which made no sense, some thirteen men and women who smiled up at them from the deep, floral furniture where they sat comfortably in their nice clothes. Brian stood beside Muriel and his father in the doorway, saying "hello." The prayer meeting was about to begin.

The mansion of Hayes Johnson was a stolid manifestation of a self-made oil man who dabbled in things religious. The large colonial with long wings sat perched atop a dark hill and was set all around with topiary crosses, each underlit by red spotlights. Hayes himself—in pale blue suit and orange tie—hugged Brian's father, then hugged Muriel, and hugged Brian. He led them to the living room, and Brian caught the extra little glance that passed between Hayes and Muriel.

An hour went by. They were all sitting on the carpet in a circle, holding hands, and it was out of a reluctance to make a scene that Brian joined them. He wondered if these people, like his father and Muriel, had learned to overcome temptation by giving in to it, by deciding that whatever they did was fine as long as they asked later to be forgiven, and asked also that their victim be forgiven because, invariably, their victim made them do it.

"Well, why don't we get started?" Hayes said. "I know, I know—I hate this part, too. But it's tithing time."

Everyone had taken out a checkbook.

"Will a thousand do?" his father laughed joyously. They all laughed in the same key. Brian glanced at the check as it passed hands toward Hayes; his father wasn't kidding. He glanced at him, but the old man wouldn't look back.

And now, all hands were joined in a circle of silence, and Hayes was praying for them all in his melodious baritone. Brian alone kept his eyes open, allowing his attention to drift over the chairs and paintings. The length of the day began to weigh on him. He was tired. The warm bath of words began to flow over him, to soothe and reassure him, and he began to feel the same sensual high of the afternoon, to enjoy the soothing smoothness of the litany. He was again a child at a railway station, alive to the warmth of the sun as he lay down among the scratchy weeds, his father's voice speaking in the air above him. "Listen to me son; I have to do this. You don't understand . . . "

"And we pray tonight, Jesus," Hayes was saying, "for young Brian here, that he may see your wisdom and know your peace of mind. He is ready, Jesus. Take him; we ask you. He is in pain and lost and confused."

Brian opened his eyes. He felt that he ought to say he wasn't that lost or confused, but he didn't.

"Do you take Jesus Christ as your savior?" Hayes said. His voice was large and kind and loving; the grave expression of his eyes said all Brian's pain would go away very soon now, with a word.

His father spoke up. "It's okay, son. Do this for me."

"Jesus," the others were saying, "love him, Jesus."

His father went on. "You don't understand, son. You can't fight Him with your mind. Trust me, son. Say 'yes,' for me. The Lord asked me to bring you here tonight. So, let me do this for you, son, please. Let me bring you to Jesus and give you eternal life."

Brian felt tired and far away from himself. "Look, Dad," he said. "I really appreciate the thought—"

"Save him, Jesus," one woman said. She raised her small, fat hands, wiggling them above her head. The others picked up the refrain. "Save him, Jesus! Save him, Jesus!" Many hands came onto Brian then, hands on his thighs, hands on his arms, hands on his back, hands on his head, hands on his hair, hands moving and persuading and soft and reassuring, and somewhere far away the voices were going on, "Save him, Jesus." But a sharp note came in, "Satan, get behind me," this last from the woman with the small, fat hands who had begun to thrust her buttocks rhythmically into the carpet, eyes closed, hands waving above her head. Brian looked through them and saw his father watching him go through this. His father had become detached, as he had been that first night in the restaurant when Muriel told him the money was for a children's hospital.

"Okay, Hayes." His father's tone was bright and clear. "I just wanted him to meet everyone, that's all. That's enough, okay?" He laughed, not joyously, but like himself again. "You all—come on, now. Son, get up. Stand up, son, just stand up—"

One of the women shrieked. The hands fell away from Brian's body. It was the woman with the fat hands. She was looking amazed, wild, her eyes astonished. "Something stung me," she said. "I was stung!" She looked frantically around her. "It was that ring." She pointed at his father's right hand. "Satan stung me from that ring!"

His father laughed joyously. "Doris, I think you've had a little too much of that communion wine."

Muriel had begun to glare at the ring. She stood and leveled her hand down between their heads. "In the name of Jesus Christ, our Savior, Satan—I command you to get thee behind me!" She aimed her accusing index finger at the ring.

"The ring stung me," the woman said. She stood up. She said it again. She shook her hand, held it out for them to see. "That ring stung me! Satan is in that ring!" A gaunt man was speaking in tongues at the ceiling. The circle was reforming. Hands began to come down on his father's back, on his thighs, arms, and head. They all began to shift and settle around his father. They were chanting, praying, commanding Jesus to get Satan behind them.

In the twilight of the living room, Brian and his father stood up, two men of average size who began to push through thirteen others toward the front door. But the others were leading his father, and Hayes was in the midst of them, urging his father outside; and it occurred to him at once that they were free to go, and were leaving, and then that they were not free to go but were being taken outside.

"Dad, I got the keys. I'll start the car." Brian jogged down the hill to the van. He popped the side door. "Okay—we got everybody? Muriel?"

Atop the hill by the garage they had formed a group in the darkness of the driveway. He could not see his father. They were chanting. With hands cupped around his mouth, he called back, "Hey, Dad, Muriel—you guys ready?" Brian started up the hill, until he could see his father standing within the group. He called again, got no answer, and found himself at a halt at the edge of the drive. Nothing seemed to be happening, and he realized that this was his father's choice. He'd thrown away his entire family for these people. But the next thought was clear in the stillness: whatever was going to happen, maybe his father deserved it.

Hayes jogged out from the garage and passed a hammer into the center of the group. The chanting died to a prayer. From his position on the lawn, aware that Muriel stood outside the group watching him watching his father, Brian heard the gold ring fall with a clink onto the asphalt. Muriel's arms were crossed. Between all those standing legs, he saw his father bend to his knees, raise the hammer, and strike it down. Brian shouted. The impact made a dull crack. No one answered. He shouted. His father raised the hammer, struck again, struck again, struck again, struck again, until Hayes restrained him, took the hammer, and passed it out of the circle. He lifted Brian's father by the armpits into his arms and hugged him. The others moved their hands over his father's back and shoulders; they were moving; it sounded like someone in the group was weeping. Muriel joined them as they moved en masse back to the front door. She kissed his father on the side of his neck. In twos and threes they crossed the red spotlights back into the house.

Brian had not moved. Now he kneeled over the dim spot in the driveway. He could pick loose only a fragment of the crest—its last initial intact. The bulk of the ring had shattered, its shards flattened onto the sun-warmed asphalt.

He came inside. The lights were bright. The living room was clean, the floral upholstery lovely. Most of the group was leaving, and talking pleasantly, if a bit anxiously, in the foyer. They hugged each other and praised Jesus for the miracle they'd seen against Satan. They were quick to leave.

"Very well, then," his father said. The strain in his face was unmistakable. This was the face of the suburban duffer harrassed and out of control and throwing cocktail glasses at his children then pretending that nothing had happened, the man kicking and swinging his fists at the sons who cowered in the closet. "We'll talk to you the first of the week, Hayes. Do lunch. My treat this time."

Muriel and the woman with fat hands were embracing each other and praising Jesus. Hayes was shaking hands all around. Brian didn't know where to look or whom to avoid; he stepped back into the living room. They all gave him an automatic, cloying good-bye, but they did not even try to kiss, hug, or shake hands with him. His father handed Brian his sport coat while the others went back outside, then put his arm around Brian's shoulders. He kept him back a moment. His father's face was close to his, the jaws closely shaven, smelling of lemon-lime; but the eyes, still puffy, were unfathomable. This was not the suburban duffer, either; this was no one he knew.

"You don't understand, son," he said. "I had to. It was evil. And don't tell your mother either, boy. It would break her heart."

IV

In the June sunlight, on another advent of summer, the silver wing of the aircraft dipped toward the sun, glazing itself with light, and swept over the highways and quadrangular city streets, the towers leaning flatly against the landscape. The flight attendant had brought him a Bloody Mary before takeoff. He had gotten up before his father, but the old man had insisted on making him breakfast. Muriel came lumping about the kitchen in her satin robe which bloused open to reveal her hanging breasts. The radio was talking about sports and weather in the sunlit silence.

"Well, I just think that Doris is getting too high on her hog for her own good," Muriel said. "I saw the sparks of lust in your eye. You can't fool me. Satan was in you—you wanted her."

"How about some more eggs, son," his father interrupted. "Some waffles? Muriel, check and see if we have any waffles left in the freezer."

Muriel looked at his father. "Well, I guess we'll have to pray a little harder now to pay the next few months' rent on that office space. I couldn't believe you wrote that check last night. And all we needed was one convert. You look—we're all out." She slammed the fridge, walked down the hallway, shut the bedroom door.

His father drove him to the airport in the left-hand lane, ahead of traffic. With the bright city receding, Brian's thoughts began to weave and connect like overpasses, but the overall view still eluded him. Some thought wouldn't take shape against the brilliance. Concrete problems came into the foreground: where to park? His father escorted him to the gate while he walked on, slightly spacing out in the airport's bright confusion of announcements and noise.

"Well, son, sure was good seeing you, and maybe I'll get to see everyone if I get to reunions this year."

"That'd be good." They shook hands, and Brian felt his father's fingers collapse where the ring had been.

"Well, Dad, I'm just sorry I ruined your chance to raise rent money last night. Guess next time I'll accept Jesus, so Hayes can pay you off. Or whatever it is you guys do."

His father stepped back and turned away, visibly appalled, then looked at him again. "Oh, son. You can't believe I would do such a thing. Is it something Muriel said? 'Cause you can't listen to her. She's not right in the head."

"What was that about lust, Dad? Was she joking?"

"Oh, god, son, don't even ask. The last time she screamed at me for five days and tried to exorcise me. I don't even want to go back there."

"Then don't."

"You don't understand, son. I have to."

Brian straightened up and looked at the line of people having their tickets checked at the door. "Well, good luck with that. Good seeing you again."

His father clapped him on the back, pulled him into a hug, then let go. Brian moved slowly on, to his seat with a view of the aircraft's wing.

"Would you like another?" the attendant said. The man seated across the aisle—sixties, dark suit—said, "Yes."

The plane beveled out against the tonic brilliance of the eastern
sun, an orange hemisphere of the planet roaring with engines. They
rose steeply, then the seatbelt light went off with the tone of a bell.
The plane was banking, and in the cool of the morning, Brian's eyes
traced the intricate street connections between the millions below,
that steel cluster being his father's office building, and somewhere in
the azure distance, the condo complex and, invisible now, the hill
upon which sat Hayes' house.

"Would you like another?"

Sunlight came down the wing and boomed across the window,
flashing as the aircraft shuddered. Brian turned—the attendant was
pretty, breasty, and healing—but he could barely say "yes." A thought
coming to him from beyond the window would not take shape in
words. The city design below had just been legible, but what he now
saw in his mind was the driveway of last night, the group, the ham-
mering, the way Muriel had stood watching him. Had she sacrificed
his father? He put his hand to his temple, closed his eyes. Had his father tried to sacrifice him? Neither one. He had done it to his father.

"Would you like some chewing gum?" the attendant said.

He shook his head, no, but asked for another drink.

He had done it when he said "hello"; he had done it when he
thought only of himself and of the estate; he had done it when he had-
n't interfered, when he failed to look at some element in the picture
other than himself, oil derricks, and deceit. He had done it when he
said "good luck."

Across the aisle the man in the dark suit was turning pages in a
weekly news magazine.

"You poor bastard," Brian said quietly.

The man looked up, as if he had heard something.

Brian looked back out the window. It was stupid; it was crazy; but
it was who they were and who they would be, just as there were city
streets somewhere down there beneath that orange bath of pollution.
He reminded himself that this was only his understanding of things,
but it didn't seem to matter anymore. Their decisions had been made
for them. His father was right: he didn't understand. When he got
home he would talk to his siblings—Stuart, Jay, and Moriah—tell
them what had happened, and together they would hire the lawyers.

|||||||| If I Were You

I

AS THE TAXI CARRIED ME THROUGH THE NIGHT, I KEPT STARING into the streams of headlights, wondering how I would handle this. All I had was a first name—Hugh or Stew—and a poorly developed mental picture of the young navy pilot who had proposed unsuccessfully to my mother more than three decades ago. To his face I had added some flesh to account for those years, but I could not yet imagine calling him Father or see myself shaking hands with his clan, a new family of half-brothers and -sisters.

The taxi stopped. Edgewood Avenue was asleep. The St. John's was surging beneath the stars, and the carriage lamps at the door were bright—a normal scene. But as I got out into the balmy darkness of the Floridian winter, set my suitcase down, and paid the driver, I had no idea that within the next few days he would try to poison me for loving his daughter—the navy pilot, that is, not the cab driver.

And yet, the funny thing is that I'm not the sort to go looking for his real father, like those people you see on TV who, having been separated for twenty years, throw themselves into some tearful Waltons' reunion. That stuff always makes me cringe. And the camera crew never sticks around for what must surely follow: the lull that comes when the strangers find each other a bit depressing. So, that was my credo: stay away from scenes of family drama. But then one night back at Thanksgiving, when my older sister and I were on a quick run to Davidson's, she happened to tell me that she had found a love letter.

"And passion isn't the word for it, Stuart. And you want to know what page it was on? Lanie, come here."

My three-year-old niece came trotting down the aisle toward us, waving her tiny hands for balance.

"It was signed Hugh or Stew, I think."

"What were you doing, reading Mom's diary?"

"Lanie, put that back. Good girl. No, I was making room in the bookcase. Give up? The day you were born. Your birthday, Stuart. A love letter. And passion isn't the word for it. I think she was having an affair."

I came to a full stop by the canned peas and looked at my shoes. The linoleum tiles began melting into currents at the end of which stood my tall, laughing sister. "Well, at least it wasn't the milkman," and she told Lanie to select a can of stewed tomatoes.

Moriah's little joke among the canned goods might have fallen away, but it didn't because I had also looked into my mother's diary. Our mother has always walked backwards through life, mourning for the world and people disappearing behind her; and one afternoon, while I was watching television in the library before doing my ninth-grade English assignment, a row of her datebooks came into focus among the bookshelves. I took down the one with the year of my birth printed on the spine and let it fall open.

The letter I set aside. Then began to read. "We came upstairs and got into bed," my mother wrote. "'Well,' he said, drunk, 'thank God for a sexless marriage.'"

I slammed the book shut, back into its slot, and watched a *Lost in Space* rerun with open-eyed horror. Even so, the chance that my father might be another man never occurred to me until the night Moriah made her little joke.

"You realize," I went on, "that you're full of shit. You're not even funny. How dare you question my paternity?"

"Sshh." She covered Lanie's ears. Lanie loved it and went trotting down the aisle, covering her ears. "Stuart, really—"

"Really what? I can't say the word 'shit,' but you can call her grandmother an adulteress and me a bastard of some kind—"

"Oh, don't be silly. You are a bastard of some kind, honey. I've always said so."

She squeezed my face between her palms and kissed the tip of my nose. Lanie stood mute, watching us.

"This is how it starts," I said. "Great—now she's going to be in therapy the rest of her life. Come here . . . " I went to pick her up, but she wailed and ran to her mother.

"Well, if I were you," Moriah said, hoisting Lanie onto her hip, "I wouldn't sweat it."

Not sweat it? I felt closer to my distraught niece than I did to my sister, for as a child I'd had that same experience—I'd seen my mother kiss another man's nose in public. But mine was an experience of ineffable happiness: an endless Sunday afternoon we spent by the Delaware River, the warm hours of sunlight drifting over the October crowds at the Lambertville flea market, the exotic and floral hippies swarming to music and motorcycles through the village streets of New Hope, and then the picnic itself at a plank-board table shining in the sensuous light of changing leaves, all of us flying above the surface of the grass as we chased the frisbee; and as we began to leave, my mother clasped uncle Jason's face between her hands and gave him a kiss on the end of his nose, and I looked away as he shut his eyes and his masculine hands took hold of her hips.

We arrived home at night. The house sat dark, but the open door threw a rectangle of light around the figure of my father, who stood with a glass in his hand. It was the house my mother had always hated, always a place that was cold and dark.

"So, everybody had a good time. Isn't that wonderful," he said. "I suppose you forgot the groceries. There's not a goddamn thing in the house."

He might as well have taken a ball-peen hammer to a figurine of spun glass. The joyous brilliancy of the afternoon shattered and fell raining into the canyon silence of the driveway.

"We picked up a few things," Uncle Jason told our father. "All set and ready to go, aren't we, kids?" And each of us carried in a bag of groceries.

There was no fight that night, no screaming, no smashing of cocktail glasses or slamming of doors. But, in the weeks after Uncle Jason left, I would mope along behind my mother, watching other children in the A&P and wondering why I couldn't be a part of their family.

"You think that letter was from Uncle Jason?"

Years later we stood in the check-out line, a pair of adult siblings, and unloaded the basket.

"You mean that he signed himself Hugh or Stew? And that he's your real father, Uncle Jason? God, Stuart, I don't know. But what you ought to do is ask Granelle."

And so my flight to Jacksonville, ostensibly to find the lawyers we would need to sue our father, who had jilted us of our inheritances. But I was too distracted with memories of playing spy and old rumors about Uncle Jason to hire anyone just yet. Old Granelle led me in, out of the windy darkness of the porch and into the warm TV room. And when I set my suitcase down in the foyer, I hoped that she would help me get out of these backwaters and reach the great wide ocean of the truth—silly as that may sound.

"So, what about it?" I said. "Same guy or what?"

Gingerly, attentively, Granelle was picking at her black-eyed peas with the tines of her fork. "Wasn't that Hardwick boy, was it? He died in Korea."

"Didn't say. Another beer. You want one?" In the kitchen I popped the fridge. "He ever propose? Give her the ring?"

"Now, Stuart, I want you to answer me one simple question. Did you come down here to see me, or did you get fired again? That's three jobs in two years. You are going on thirty years old. You cannot go on doing this. Oh, there you are. I'll have a little of yours, if you don't mind."

"Come on, Granelle, same guy or what?"

"It wasn't serious, whoever it was."

"That's not what I asked."

"Your mother is very Platonic. Now, Stuart, don't you think it's time you got married? There are plenty of women out there. You are far too old to be going on this way—"

"Are we in the same room? I ask 'A,' she answers 'Z.' Why can't I get a straight answer? Come on, Granelle, this is driving me up the wall."

"I don't see why it should bother you in the least."

Falling into my stuffed chair, I exhaled. "I can't stand mysteries, Granelle. I can't stand not knowing who I am."

She looked puffy with offense. "Well, I can't help you, if you don't want to listen."

Silence. The TV babbled. To find yourself rolling around in a conversational mud-wrestling match with your grandmother is so humiliating that I can't tell you how it felt.

"I know what let's do." She pushed herself carefully up from the armchair. "Let's us, you and me, go to that debutante ball at the Yacht Club tomorrow night."

I threw my head back and groaned at the ceiling. My mind said to call and change my reservation. My body said the phone was in the kitchen.

"Well, no one's making you," she said, picking her way along with her cane, "but you might find out who your real father is, and, if you're lucky, you might even meet a nice, single young girl." She gave a toss of her eyebrows that said, "Ah, ha!"

"Ha, ha, ha," I said, sarcastically. And in the morning called to change my reservation.

II

"Granelle, you look wonderful! Now, which grandson is this? So good to meet chuuuuuu!"

There is always an occasion before you lose a job when a lull falls over the entire office, and you notice something's up when the people you work with avoid you as if your failure were a contagion; you know for sure when you ask to borrow a pen and the look in your secretary's eye is inappropriately sad. Well, that's how I felt as I escorted Granelle from the Mercedes up the red carpeted staircase into the Yacht Club—an occasion when your stupidity gets trapped behind your smile. Handshakes beneath the chandelier of the Spanish foyer, and then, sturdy as a dowager duchess, she led me on through anterooms ablaze with decorations and into the roaring ballroom where lights were flickering over hundreds of people.

Frat boys were braying hog-calls at each other, and sorority girls were bustling into the women's room. Businessmen as bulky as oil burners yanked each other's hands, their wives sweeping by in flocks of sequins. The debutantes had not yet been escorted down the runway by their fathers, but that would come: a tribal cattle auction for the young financial studs. The evolutionary battle of spermatozoa for the egg lifted to the level of community theater. God, to be there at my age—I felt unmoored by the spectacle, the loss of my job, and my fiscal pipsqueakery among the upper bourgeoisie.

And yet the sad part of the evening was that I did not yet know the story behind the navy pilot and the love letter, and I would not know it until the next night when Moriah filled me in.

"Oh, God, Stuart," Moriah said the next night over the phone. "If I tell you about that letter, you can't repeat it to anyone, ever. Promise me. You have to promise."

Seated on the bed, battered, I rubbed my face and promised.

"Okay, it was back before Mom met Dad. She and Rosaline Sherman were close friends, and Rosaline was wild about this handsome young navy pilot. So she threw this big house party at the beach, but the minute he gets there he sees Mom and instantly starts talking to her. And they wind up spending the entire party together as if no one else was there. And, as Mom puts it, they became 'very close very fast.' Everyone was talking about them because they were such a couple. And Rosaline was furious. She felt like Mom had stolen him but there was nothing she could do."

"Now, Stuart," Granelle said to me at the Yacht Club party. I was gazing across the dance floor. "Stuart, you know Rosaline Sherman, don't you? They live just down from me on Edgewood."

Rosaline squeezed my hand affectionately. "Your mother and I are old friends. We used to date the same boys!"

She and Granelle laughed, and I went back to scanning the roaring darkness of the ballroom. Because Moriah hadn't told me about the letter yet, I didn't look closely at Rosaline, but I got a quick take— tall, starved, and painted, her features gone Art Deco with age. As if she had once modeled for *Vogue*.

"So, anyway," Moriah went on, "the navy pilot gets transferred to Baltimore, but he and Mom write letters—long love letters to each other all the time. Then Rosaline flies up to Baltimore for a debutante party, and she finds him and she tells him that Mom is in love with someone else, about to be engaged, and that he's the laughing stock of Jacksonville for falling for her and writing her."

"Why don't you ask one of these girls to dance, Stuart?" Granelle nudged my arm, indicating a line of spinsters my age, waiting for husbands along the velvet margins of the crushing confusion between youth and old age.

"Maybe," I said. "Let me think about it."

"And then," Moriah went on, "Rosaline comes back to Jacksonville and she tells Mom that she saw him up there, the navy pilot, that he's running around with some woman he's in love with and about to be engaged to, and that she's a laughing stock for writing him all those letters.

"And all at once," Moriah said, "they stopped. That was it. The navy pilot never wrote to her again. And Mom never wrote to him again. And all because of Rosaline Sherman."

The Rosaline Sherman of thirty-five years later kissed Granelle on the cheek and waved goodbye as she walked into the crowd, and that was the last I saw of her.

"Now, Stuart," Granelle said. "You, Stuart! Pay attention here a moment. I want to introduce you to someone."

The post-presentation pandemonium on the dance floor was distracting, but I turned to the young woman who stood beside Granelle. She held her drink with both hands, one beneath the other—quite an attractive young woman, late twenties, dark blond hair, short black evening dress, long, pretty legs in dark, sheer stockings.

"Nicole's studying at Oxford this year, aren't you?"

Now she came into focus. Ash gold hair woven into a thick French braid, clipped with a black bow, a style both casual and formal enough to outline the heart shape of her face. She gave me a smile with only her eyes, and I saw the Florentine curl of her mouth. Our eyes met. Her irises were green and gold. And in that moment the entire room drifted back into silent abstraction.

"Your grandmother tells me you're a paralegal in Washington but you're going to law school," Nicole said. "That's wonderful. I have a number of friends on the hill. Tell me, Stuart, is it really such a soap opera up there?"

She said my name! The sound of her voice speaking my name felt like a soul-filling kiss, an intimate touch like the brush of her cheek against mine, a glimpse of her heavy-lidded eyes through a bedroomish fall of hair. Granelle started going on about her favorite soaps, and I stood there, dazed, as if I was not myself but someone else. Nicole kept me involved with a few inclusive smiles, however, and I had never seen another woman of our generation manage such a moment so gracefully.

"But years later," Moriah went on, "they did see each other a few more times, in New York. It was the year before you were born, Stuart. Mom and the navy pilot. And that was the letter I found. He had a wife and kids and was living in Jacksonville."

Nicole's clothes spoke of New York shopping trips, her poise of the sort of timeless patrician confidence that unfolded the landscape of a half-remembered life. That was her country, after all, a world of advantages and wealth—not some junkyard pitched with a sign that reads, "I Can't" or "I Don't Know How." Granelle would later tell me that her father was the CEO of thirteen corporations. Nicole was laughing and turned to me.

"So—speaking of outrageous kidnappings—Granelle, would you mind if I kidnapped Stuart for a while?" She laid her hand on my tuxedo forearm, and I thought I would never stop smiling.

So there we were, shagging along with hundreds of others on the parquet floor amid the whirl and blasting lights. She spun away from me and slipped out the black bow, shaking her hair in loose, sexy luxuriance all around her face—wind blown. She shouted in my ear above the descending thunder—"The vertical expression of a horizontal desire!"—and backed into the hubbub, swinging a fan of hair in wild circles and shimmying her sensuous bare shoulders at me. I spun in ecstasy. Men stood in the doorways, lusting after her. And I could not stop smiling. She came back, sweet gin breath on my mouth, shouting, "I was a floating guitarcase!" And as she went spazzing away in the strobe lights, whatever she was trying to tell me was lost forever.

Dances, drinks, a table of our own—we shouted about careers and children, where to live. We lifted each other's lips and liked what we saw: no sign of pyorrhea of the gums, emotions, or intellect. And we came together on so many subjects, liking all the same movies and books and politicians, that talking was like tracing the curve of new skin with ecstatic fingers. Nicole and I were so close that we might have been siblings, and suddenly I was free from the burden of having to know who my real father was. Now that I had met Nicole, the question of his identity no longer mattered to me. Although I was afraid to think it out this articulately, I had the familiar conviction that, having found her, I had found my whole being and reason to be.

"I'm shocked you don't remember. Or maybe insulted."

"What?" We hadn't looked at anyone else for hours.

"The first time we met, Stuart. Granelle says you went to the Atlantic Boulevard elementary school."

"Did I? Oh, that's right. Ages ago—"

"Now I'm really hurt." Nicole traced a provocative line up the slow length of her glass. "I had such a crush on you then, I wanted to marry you. Don't you remember? I was the girl who got ants in her pants and had to take them off. Remember?"

Like a flash: sunlight, sandbox, teacher, boys, girl. "That was you?"

"I told everyone you were my brother, then I said you were my husband. Isn't it funny, your mother and my father used to go out? Ah, me, fearful symmetry—"

I laughed. "Thank God they never married!"

She balanced the glass on its edge. "Why don't you come out tomorrow night for dinner? The whole family will be there, and I really want you to meet them. And I would love another drink, if you're getting one."

She gathered her hair and clipped the bow back on.

Bliss, bliss. Now it all came back—a girl in a sandbox taken from me by an army of red ants. But she was back and grown into a lovely woman. Straightening and buttoning my tux—an old one of my grandfather's, which I had put on sans gloves and spats—I shouldered between the other men at the long bar and told the bartender what we wanted.

"Oh, Stuart," Moriah said. "Oh, Stuart."

III

It was not I who drove Granelle's old Mercedes through the twilight of Atlantic Boulevard the next evening, humming along to some silly song on the radio. Nor did Granelle expect to find me at the stove that morning, scrambling an iron skillet of eggs, with grits, coffee, apples frying, and sizzling bacon permeating the modest kitchen with an aroma as strong as nostalgia. For the first time in my life, it seemed, there was no world of regret in the landscape around me, as I turned the wheel and rolled at last into the heavily forested Hadley estate in Orange Park.

I parked among a half dozen cars, including a jeep and Jag, and got out into the evening. Wind on the leaves. In the spacious park massive water oaks appeared to uphold the sky like the mammoth hands of some sunken colossus who had torn rags of Spanish moss from the earth and now held them between his fingers as down he sank. No one around. Sprinklers were clicking sprays across the lawn. Water spritzing. In the distance an outboard groaning up the river gave a hush to my footsteps across the concrete, and on the pale night came the incongruous smell of things wet and growing.

And so here I was. The mansion of decks and walls of glass and redwood, with the St. John's bending in massive silence to the unseen ocean, stood like an old family fortress before me in the last hour of dusk. Although I had not yet spoken to Moriah, I nonetheless had the acute impression that here was the world we should have grown up in. It was not dark; my father did not stand in the doorway; and yet here I was again. Each step that cracked across the acorns and twigs and kicked aside the rags of Spanish moss was a step out of my world and into the one always beside me—not-seen because not-looked-for— but heard, half heard, like the silence between two waves of the sea. It was the world of the unborn, the should-have-been. For, as I stood pressing the bell, I believed that here was a whole new set of chances before me, lost by accident but given back by miracle. I could have the life that I'd never known, after all—as her husband. Footsteps were coming down the hall. It was the seventh ring.

"You made it! Oh, don't worry about them," she said.

And I was glad she was so confident, because three English mastiffs had come out of the garage—sizes suitably overblown to fit the mansion—and I patted skulls the breadth of basketballs as they nudged and shoved me backwards into the house. We shut them outside.

Upon shutting the door, I got my first vague notion that maybe something was off. Even though I was quite cheerful, Nicole went down the hallway without a word. Wondering where the closet was, I draped my Irish tweed jacket over a Queen Anne chair by the phone table and followed her to the end of the hall, where she was pushing the sleeves of her red cashmere sweater up to her elbows and folding her arms. "The living room," she announced.

Before us lay a deep room sunk beneath cathedral timbers, walls of stone and glass, black leather sofas. Four large gold Indian elephants braced a table top of glass on their backs. And as I gazed into the stillness, the space suddenly bloomed with people and commotion: we could have the wedding reception here in August, and one day our children would play basketball in this great room, since a regulation hoop extended from the gigantic granite blocks of the hearth.

"We're big on games," Nicole said, almost morosely.

She looked behind me, and I became aware that an argument was going on among several people in the kitchen. But, as if to distract me, she drew back the glass door. "Let me show you the boat," she said somberly, and here I went first, stepping into the river light of evening. We went down through the gardens to the river and, I hoped, to our lives together.

For an hour we were on the dock in the wind and silence of the St. John's, in the presence of their canvas-wrapped, three-masted yacht, sixty-three feet long because it was Daddy's sixty-third birthday present. That sort of annoyed me, but you learn to adapt. And besides, her mood kept me off balance—since all the romance of the previous night seemed either to have chilled in the winter daylight or to have dissipated with the champagne in her system.

And so I listened, to learn what the hell was going on. Nicole told me that it was hard to come home, and I said that family stuff shouldn't matter at our age. "I like your family," she said, sadly, and I wondered why, since hers looked so great. But this was her world and so I quit chattering and joking, and soon we were silent and the shadows of the trees and the river purling beneath the boards all spoke to us of the failing light of the world, of things alive and growing as they always have. Nicole raised her hands to the sky and brought them behind her head, lifting her lovely face toward the clouds of sunset underlit with pink. And that's how I will always remember her, in the last moments of light, when we seemed to have the lives we wanted—only moments before I met her family of outrageous bastards. And yet, when we still didn't go in to supper, I began to wonder if I should leave.

"Well, it's getting late."

"Why don't you stay for supper?" She took me by the hand, her fingers laced between mine. "It's no problem, really." And I tried to unscramble the signals all the way back up to the house.

Four people were grouped around a cooking island in the enormous kitchen, and though I knew nothing of their behavior as a family, I had the sense that a subject got dropped as we came in; certainly a spoon did. They each glanced away, then came into my face with hellos and handshakes so boisterous you could feel the insincerity they were trying to conceal. Some of this was just Southern, but I still wondered if I shouldn't take off, as we sat at a kitchen table so large it had places for sixteen.

"So," Mrs. Hadley said, as we all sat down, "what do you think of our refrigerators?"

I'd been watching Nicole's mother, trying to imagine how she would have aged if she had had to sell real estate rather than play tennis. So, I looked at the banks of stainless steel doors with appreciation. "Looks like you run a restaurant."

"Daddy, what are you doing with the eggrolls? Daddy, let me do them—" Helene, the eldest, stood up.

"Why, I've never in my life! Have you ever seen anything like it?" Mrs. Hadley popped her eyes at me. "Nicole, pinch me if I'm awake—"

"Dad's going faggot," said the brother, Aubrey, a muscular college frat boy who came back in and crashed down in his chair.

The CEO of thirteen corporations, wrapped in a powder blue apron, stood at the cooking island trying to fry egg rolls in a wok.

"Not once in thirty-one years of marriage have I ever seen your father do one thing in the kitchen. He must be showing off for you, Stuart—"

"Daddy!" Helene bolted, knocking back her chair.

A fire had burst out under the wok, and the CEO of Lockheed and General Mills, was fanning a spatula at the flames. Helene dumped baking soda on the fire and shuffled the egg rolls onto a serving plate. The acrid stench of torched grease drifted over us in shapes of blue smoke.

"Wonderful," Helene said. "They're all burned." She swung the plate down on the table with a loud clack.

"Well, that's okay," the mother said. "You don't mind them a little done, do you, Stuart? Stuart won't mind—it's a free supper, after all. Now, Hugh, I insist. Come and sit down, and let Helene finish cooking those."

"Sorry?" I said.

They all looked at me.

"Sorry . . . I mean, I didn't catch the name is all."

"I introduced you, didn't I?" Nicole said. "This is my mother, Margaret. Aubrey and Helene. And my father, Hugh. Daddy, didn't I tell you? You used to go out with Stuart's mother when you were a pilot in the navy."

The others in the room, the table, the fixtures, the faces withdrew from the foreground, and at the far end stood a young navy pilot of more than thirty years ago, the smile reserved as mine is, the nose a little aquiline, and maybe something about the mouth. And when the others went on talking, I found myself looking at a tall man in his sixties, more flesh in his face, pink glasses, yellow bow tie, tweed sports coat. Balding. Remote. Judgmental. Wrapped in a blue apron. Cooking in the wok. Trying to avoid looking at us. Or maybe just me.

"We have this wonderful Vietnamese man," the mother was telling me across Nicole, who had closed up within her own silence. "And he always wants to cook for us. And I always tell him 'No' because we just can't afford another thing, but he just loves to cook for us. So these are genuine Vietnamese egg rolls. Hope you don't mind artichoke and egg rolls."

"We don't usually eat like this, " Nicole said toward her lap, and in a glance I saw the resemblance between us—the same nose in profile, the same curly hair; and glancing around the table now, I saw this resemblance in both Helene and Aubrey.

"Only when Dad the faggot cooks, " Aubrey was saying, and he either didn't notice or chose to ignore the frown Nicole gave him.

We dug in. A moment passed during which our six jaws of teeth cracked and crunched into the blackened cases of the egg rolls. And I was glad for the distraction because my mind had slipped into a kind of very quiet hysteria. I had come here because I was wild about Nicole, but now if Mr. Hadley was my real father then that meant that Nicole was . . . no, no, no—Moriah had said "Hugh or Stew." I kept telling myself that. It had to be Stew.

"So," Mr. Hadley said. "Nicole tells me you're a freelance writer. Who do you write for?"

I could hardly look at him. "Well, not really—"

"It's a hard life," the mother said. "You have to have talent."

"Well, uh, I did write for a newspaper on Martha's Vineyard."

"Helene's a writer," Mrs. Hadley said. "We used to own that paper."

"Really? Who do you write for? What paper?"

"*TV Guide*," the mother went on. "And her husband is a producer, Junghans Weir. Ever see the show *L.A. Blues*? That's his. And he has a movie in development. They're trying to get Bruce Willis and Julia Roberts." She took a mouthful.

"*TV Guide*," I said. Her husband's name rang a faint bell. But I went on. "That's great. How do they pay?"

This gaucherie was part of the way freelancers kibbitz when they meet, but when Helene raised her eyes at me, she didn't look especially pleased.

"I haven't written for a newspaper, ever," she said.

Bunched over his plate and chewing, Mr. Hadley glared at me. "What did you say your name was again? Oh, yes—I knew your father at Princeton. A wonderful man, your father. I always felt for him. He could have had a wonderful career, but it was ruined by a bad marriage."

I was stunned. He had dated my mother and he said that? I was so poleaxed that not a word came to mind, and I felt myself sort of collapse, like my empty jacket out in the hallway.

"So, what do you want to do with your life, young man? Well? Any ideas?"

"Uhh, well—not really. I mean, I'm thinking of law school, sort of, but only sort of. Not seriously."

"Granelle told me you were going to Yale," Nicole said.

"Ah, yes, well, thinking of it!" I said, and felt this odd sensation as she looked back at her plate—as though something had been taken back, like the pressure of a hand, the protection of her respect. Helene was standing at the island, uncorking a bottle of wine, and asked if I would like a glass. But I was swallowing lettuce and shrimp and astonishment just then and couldn't answer.

"He's a heliophile," Helene said. "Aren't you?"

"Sorry?" I said.

"Heliophile," she said. "I don't think he knows what it means." She got the cork out.

"Do you know what it means?" the mother asked me.

When I confessed that I didn't, Mr. Hadley spoke through a mouthfull of well-chewed mash. "It's a well-known fact," he said with irritation, "that artichoke leaves will ruin the palate for a fine wine. That's one of the first things I ever learned!"

I looked at the artichoke seated on my plate, so much like the de-capitated head of a porcupine, and was honest about my ignorance. "How do you eat this thing anyway?"

"You've never had artichoke!" Aubrey bellowed. "Man, where have you been?"

"New Jersey," I said, rather cool.

"Well," Mr. Hadley said, munching away, "you take a leaf, dip it in butter, then put the whole thing in your mouth, chew it up, and swallow."

Instructions like that make you feel rather stupid, but not as stupid as I felt a moment later as I chewed the tough, pointed leaf.

"I can't believe he did that!" Aubrey blasted the table with the palm of his hand.

"Daddy!" Nicole said. "I can't believe you told him to do that! He said he's never had one before!"

"What?" I managed to say, and raised my water glass to my mouth.

"You just scrape it with your teeth," Nicole said. "The whole leaf is poisonous."

I swallowed some water, leaf, and prayer, then picked the spine from my molars and wiped it on my plate. Not even my own father would have done that. Not one of them would look at me. They were absorbed in eating their food.

"I'm sorry he's being such a jerk tonight," Nicole said. "Daddy, he's my guest. I still can't believe you did that."

"Daddy's rather droll sometimes," Helene said.

"Funny's more like it," Aubrey said.

"Still," Helene went on, "you'd think a journalist would be more observant."

In my silence I felt a sensation of gathering unto myself, of all the men inside me compounding weapons and fortifications. And while the Hadleys picked apart the artichokes and me with equal relish, I decided to rise above them all. And to be a good sport, I did scrape some of the savorless pap onto my teeth before shoving the thing away.

"You don't like artichoke?" Mrs. Hadley's tone was edged with accusation.

"I don't dislike it," I said.

"That's a litotes," Helene said, chewing vigorously.

"Yes, litotes," the mother said. "Do you know what litotes is?"

"I don't know what it is," Nicole said, and I had the disheartening feeling she was coming to my rescue.

"And you went to Yale!" the mother said.

"It's like a double negative," I said.

"It's not like a double negative at all" Mrs. Hadley snapped ferociously.

"Well, I mean, it's like a 'not-un' phrase."

"Yes, that's right," she said, with a patronizing smile.

For a nanosecond, I wouldn't say it, but then realized it was something my own father would say, so I did say it. "As in, 'He is not unwelcome.'"

Silence. Then Aubrey looked at me from his end of the table. "Nicole says you went to Vassar. She's under the impression that you studied with Henry MacKenner."

"As an undergraduate," I said. "Only a course or two."

"No, you didn't," Aubrey said.

"What?"

"You didn't study with Henry MacKenner."

I laughed. "Yes, I did!"

"No, you didn't. He teaches at Gainesville. He's not at Vassar."

Now I felt grounded. "Well, he may have taught there or lectured there, but he's been at Vassar, on tenure, for twenty-some years now."

"No, he hasn't. Henry MacKenner, the Pound and Yeats expert? He teaches at Gainesville."

"I know who I studied with," I said, with the warmth of liquid nitrogen.

"You're obviously thinking of the other Henry MacKenner," Aubrey said. "There are two Henry MacKenners."

"It's surprising to think he wouldn't know whom he studied with," Helene said to her plate.

"Exactly! " I said.

"When I was at Harvard," she went on, "I knew who my professors were."

I exhaled and lowered my fork to my plate. "Look," I said, "for twenty-some years now, Hank MacKenner has—"

"See," Aubrey interrupted, "you said 'Hank'! I'm talking about Henry. You studied with the other one."

"Stop!" the mother said. She clapped her hands at both of us. "Stop, stop, stop, stop, stop! Now just stop. This is silly, boys. We're never going to resolve this. Let's just say you're both right. Really, this is so silly it reminds me of Pirandello."

Helene raised an inquiring eyebrow.

"Oh, come on," I said, playfully. "Surely, you've heard of Pirandello."

Helene lowered her eyes at me and looked as though she were squinting into a missile sight. "Who was Pirandello?" she said.

I faltered, then tried a casual dodge. "Plays third base for the Yankees." No one laughed but me.

Helene leaned closer. "Who was Pirandello?"

I leaned back as if to get out of the crosshairs. But there were adamantine faces all around me, walling me in, so I stood up and walked right into whatever she had. Even so, I raised my water glass for the casual touch. "He did those seven views of Rome."

Explosion—laughter blasting the table—but not Nicole. Aubrey beat the table with a rhythm that made the dishes chatter.

"Piranesi," he shouted. "Even I knew that one!"

Very quietly Nicole said, "We're big on games, remember?"

"Pirandello was an Italian playwright," Helene said, as they all subsided. "He wrote the play *Six Characters in Search of an Author.*"

"Oh, that's right," I said. "And didn't he also write the sequel, *Six People in Search of Character?*"

Everyone was silent.

Nicole said, "Mom, I think Stuart's mother was in your class at Vassar."

"Oh, yes." Mrs. Hadley remembered her now. "Such a social butterfly, your mother, always carrying on with a string of men. And you have a grandmother, Granelle, and don't you have a summer place in the mountains—"

"Just like the Waltons!" Aubrey labored the table with his fist .

My mouth fell ajar, and I simply stared at him.

"You know what I'd like to see," Aubrey went on. "You put all the Waltons on board the *Saratoga*! Can you see them?" He spat and spluttered an explosion between his lips, lifting his hands into a dome above his plate, as if it were the surface of the ocean. He caught me watching him, with what must have been the look of an appalled anthropologist. "The *Saratoga*?" he said, belligerently. "Pearl Harbor? World War II ring a bell?"

"Vaguely," I said.

Mr. Hadley glared up at me, dragging an artichoke leaf between his fangs. "How can you call yourself a writer if you don't know anything about military history?"

"Good question," I shot back. "Next time I see John Keats, I'll have to ask him what he remembers about Pearl Harbor!"

"Who?" Aubrey spat a leaf onto his plate.

"John Keats," I said. "Outfielder for the Giants."

"The Giants are a football team," Aubrey said, and while he laughed for his father's approval, I lost all my patience with him, and with all of them.

"So, Chip," I said. "You're in high school, eh? Isn't that swell. And what grade are you in?"

Silence. If someone had dropped a wish just then it would have landed with a noise like thunder. As it happened, I did drop a wish: to God, to Mr. Wizard, to anyone who could get me out of there. But I also sent a little note of thanks upward—for letting me grow up with a father who had taught me to fight with my verbal fists.

Mrs. Hadley spoke coldly. "Aubrey happens to be dyslexic, but that doesn't mean he cannot read. And he is in his second year at Gainesville, for your information."

For the duration of the next egg roll, I retreated into myself, huddling for relief somewhere back against my spine, curled up beside a rib, licking my wounds but oddly exhilarated by dimensions of the fight that I couldn't understand. If for a while I was afraid to return to the gunslots of my pupils and take up arms again, I also felt that Nicole was back here with me.

"Well, I can't stand Barbie dolls," Helene was saying.

"Oh, I agree," the mother said. "I think they're absolutely pernicious. I wouldn't let any of you girls have one." She turned to me. "Do you know what a Barbie doll is?"

I snorted with exasperation.

"My wife is talking to you, son."

"Yes, I know what a Barbie doll is!"

"Do you have a sister?"

"Yes, I have a sister!"

"Well, then," Mrs. Hadley said. "You grew up with Barbie dolls."

I clacked my spoon in the ice cream bowl. "No, I did not grow up with Barbie dolls, thank you!"

"I didn't mean you, personally, but your sister played with them."

"No, she did not!"

"What did she play with—trucks?" Aubrey could really amuse himself.

"She and I played catch in the backyard."

Aubrey was laughing at the great joke he saw coming in his mind. "And then one day you cracked her in the head with a baseball bat and changed her personality forever, right? Right, Dad?" He blasted a big laugh.

"You have to get used to us," the mother told me across Nicole's profile, which was gazing morosely into her plate. "When you have so many intellectuals at the table all at once, the arguing can be quite— oh, *je ne sais quoi*."

"Ah, yes," I said. "I've always felt that a fine dinner conversation should have a certain *quelle heure est-il*."

Aubrey's face went blank. "Do you know what you just said?"

"He obviously doesn't speak French, either," Helene said.

"Well," the mother went on in a philosophical tone, "that's just because he was bopped in the terracotta."

"I was what?" I said.

"Born in Dakota," she said.

All I could do was tick my spoon against my bowl. I was not born in Dakota, not smothered in dolls, not a heliotrope, and I was not Letitia. But I did for a fact know who I was, where I was from, who my parents were, who my family was, what I did and did not want now and forever more, amen—though I was beginning to feel just a bit like I'd been bopped in the terracotta.

Mr. Hadley threw his cloth napkin into his empty bowl and stood up. "I'm going to read," he said, and walked out with that last amenity serving as a "nice to have met you" and "goodbye" all at once.

Aubrey beat the table. "That means he's going to put on a dress!"

With my capacity for surprise almost completely gone, I was surprised by how fast they fled the table; in fact, Nicole and I were alone by the second I straightened my knees and shook out my slacks. She walked me out to the door, silent. I swung on my grandfather's Irish tweed jacket and filled it out again.

"You'll have to come back," she said. "You will. We're not really like this. I feel horribly about tonight, I really do. If you're here in May you can come to the reception."

"Oh, really?" I said. "Ha! Well, tell Aubrey I said 'Congratulations.'"

She tilted her head slightly. "It's not Aubrey," she said. "Didn't Granelle tell you? I'm engaged. I'm getting married."

With a glance at my shoes currents began flowing, but I was sick of them, and galvanized by the fight, I looked at her again. Nicole leaned with one hand on the door frame, her face ineffably sad, and I knew suddenly that she was more lost than I was.

"You know, the funny thing is," I said, "we could have had wonderful children."

Her movement was over before I could back off, but my face was between her two palms and her lips on the tip of my nose, and in spite of myself my eyes closed and my hands took hold of her hips.

Out in the darkness I unlocked my car. The front door made a rectangle of light around Nicole's lovely silhouette. Then a second door opened inside the garage. The voice was Aubrey's and, though I couldn't distinguish the words, I didn't have to. The howls of three dogs came from the darkness along with a fierce scrabbling of nails over the concrete. I was in my car so I didn't care, but their faces battered fangs against the glass, and I felt the thudding chomp of teeth on the fenders as I tugged on the headlights. Nicole opened the door further, clapping her hands. "Stop, stop, stop," she cried, calling them back no doubt so I could drive out of the estate without accidentally hitting one of them.

"Well, I'm surprised they would act that way," Granelle said about the dinner-brawl, "and he is *not* the CEO of thirteen corporations. I never told you any such thing!" That's when I called Moriah.

"Look, why can't I ever get a straight answer? Just tell me—did they ever see each other again or what? Mom and the navy pilot. Believe me, after tonight, I have got to know—"

"Well," Moriah went on, "years and years went by and Mom was with Dad out in San Diego, and they bumped into each other. The navy pilot. He was married and had kids, and they all decided to go out for dinner.

"And Dad and the other woman were totally upset because Mom and this guy leaned across the table and started talking to each other as if they'd never been apart. And it was just like always with them. They talked and laughed and had all these inside jokes, and Dad and this other woman were terribly upset because Mom and this guy were so clearly in love and perfect for each other. And that's when they found out what Rosaline had done."

"I don't believe it," I said. "They didn't write, they didn't call—"

"Mom said you didn't make long distance calls back then, and her feelings were so hurt that she couldn't make herself write to him. And he felt the same way. He was so hurt he couldn't bring himself to write to her."

"Jesus Christ," I said. "Rosaline Sherman. I mean, I just met her last night—"

"Well, she's not stopped apologizing. Rosaline is still so upset by what she did that every time she seems Mom she apologizes, and it's been thirty-some years at least. And that's what they were having that tête-à-tête about last Christmas. Rosaline was apologizing."

"Okay, but look. About the pilot, I have to know—"

"Wait, Stuart," Moriah said. "I'm getting there. So they wrote each other a few more times. Mom and Dad were really on the rocks by then—when I was, like, two or three—and she thought having another child might save the marriage. So Mom and the pilot started to write to each other again. And talk about passion. They met in New York once or twice. The year before you were born. Years before Brian and Jay. And that's what the letter was about. He had a wife and kids in Jacksonville."

"Jesus Christ," I said. "Mr. Hadley, Aubrey—all of them! And Nicole my sister? No wonder they attacked me. They must have known! I mean, I had my doubts, but still—"

"Oh, Stuart," Moriah said. "You can't think that. Mom never saw the pilot again, because he died of a brain tumor the year you were born."

Granelle was snoring in front of late-night television when I pulled the front door shut behind me. Edgewood Avenue was asleep. Street lights and wind on the leaves, a pleasant night for a walk to the river, so I stepped out from under the red and blue lights of the old brass lantern. As I came along the bamboo forest of the Shermans' riverfront estate, I felt like going up, ringing the bell, and demanding an explanation. But for what? I still didn't know if the navy pilot was my father or where it would get me if I did know. And besides, their dogs were pacing nervously through the leaves behind the fence.

For an hour I stood on the retaining wall beneath the volume of stars, listening to water slap the bulkhead, and the view was an old and familiar one—the incandescent city rising in towers on the river of lights. And there were the lights of the Yacht Club, and of Atlantic Boulevard near Bubsy's old condo, and of the dining room table at home, and I was writing my first letter to Nicole, saving my job, and launching the law suit against our crazy father—here, here, and here —all happening at once; and it no longer worried me that everything was up to me. And feeling myself flying over the river, and alive to all the depths above and below me on this night and a million others, I decided that Here was where I would begin, then turned and walked back to the house.

LIBRARY OF CONGRESS CATALOGING-IN-PUBLICATION DATA

Chenoweth, Avery.

Wingtips: stories / by Avery Chenoweth.

p.   cm.—(Johns Hopkins, poetry and fiction)

ISBN 0-8018-6023-7 (alk. paper)

I. Title. II. Series.

PS3553.H3499W56   1998

813'.54—dc21   98-19492

                                        CIP